THE MATCHMAKER'S SECRET

Make Me A Match

KAY LYONS

KINDRED SPIRITS PUBLISHING

Chapter 1

Marsali Jones looked in the mirror and gave herself an affirming nod. The outfit she'd chosen screamed business, and so long as she didn't look at her debit account, she wouldn't scream at what she'd paid for it out of her carefully planned monthly budget. Coming across as a professional was a need, not a want. Right?

The low heels, brown slacks, and rose-gold top paired exceedingly well with the Chanel jacket she'd purchased secondhand off of a resale site, and perfected the image she'd worked to achieve over the last eight years. And now that her career was finally—finally!—taking off, well, a little splurge was okay.

"Are you ready, Ms. Jones?"

Marsali nodded and gave herself a final once-over in the mirror before following the headset-wearing associate from the green room to the wings of the nationally televised studio. Her nerves kicked up multiple levels and she inhaled, then counted slowly as she exhaled.

She'd had her doubts about appearing on this particular show because of the host's penchant for drama, but free publicity was free publicity, and she couldn't afford to pay for the exposure this interview would bring. So long as she stayed calm, cool, and collected, nothing could go wrong. Right?

"And now our special guest will give us all the insight we need to date in the twenty-first century," the host said, smiling into the camera. "Please welcome professional matchmaker and author of the bestselling *Good Girl's Guide to Dating*, Marsali Jones!"

Marsali's pulse raced as she crossed the shiny floor, praying all the while she didn't slip in the heels and go tumbling down like a drunken spring-breaker. She shook hands with the host she'd met backstage before the show had begun taping and waved to the audience before taking her appointed seat.

"Wow. Marsali, I have to say, when they said I'd

be interviewing a matchmaker, I expected someone much older and dowdy. I didn't expect our matchmaker to be so beautiful, did you, audience?"

Marsali smiled and murmured a soft word of thanks, uncomfortable with the catcalls and whistles from the audience.

"I've been looking forward to this segment all morning, Marsali. I can't wait to hear your recommendations for dating. I'm recently single, as I told you backstage, and I'm ready to jump into things again."

"Thank you, Gwen. I do have suggestions, and I certainly hope I can answer any questions you might have."

"So tell us—if we've been off the dating scene for a while, how do we start? Where do we start?"

"Both of those are easy. Start where you are. A trip to the grocery store, the gym, a walk in the park. So often we have our head down and earbuds in and we don't notice those around us, but there's a lot of potential out there if we pay attention."

"There are some cuties at my gym. Watch out, boys!" Gwen said, earning another audience laugh. "But where else? What about online dating?"

"Personally, I think we need to dial things back a notch. In our world of technology, romance has gotten lost in swipes and ghosting. If there's someone you're interested in, why not phone them and talk to them in person? Make it more personal by asking them for coffee or dinner. But keep the phones tucked away while you have a real conversation and sincerely invest in getting to know them."

"But what about our introverts out there? How do they strike up a conversation? Or is that where your matchmaking service comes into play?"

"Well, it certainly can come into play. Match-making is an age-old profession, and I'm thrilled to say that Marsali's Matches has a ninety-two-percent success rate."

"Oh, really?" Gwen said, giving the audience a wide smile. "For clarification, you're based here in Wilmington, North Carolina, but you are national?"

"Yes. I have many clients all over the US."

"Tell us how you got into the profession."

Marsali forced herself to inhale so her voice wouldn't reveal the nerves racking her. "Match-making is something I've always had a knack for. I fixed up friends in high school and college, and when I graduated with a business degree and looked at what I wanted to do, it just made sense to stick with something I love."

"How wonderful. The Wilmington area is largely single, is it not?"

"Yes, Wilmington is about sixty percent single mostly due to the colleges, but also because so many flock to the coast when they feel in need of a fresh start, whether it's after a breakup or being widowed or divorced."

"Who hires you? More men or women?"

"It's fairly even, actually. People today have busy lives and work long hours. If they aren't into bars and clubs, which skew to the younger set, they aren't sure where to go to meet people. I help with that and do a bit of investigating before they ever get to the first date."

"Investigating? That sounds interesting! Tell us more."

"Of course. I take my clients' safety seriously, and I run background checks on any potential date as well as my clients so there aren't any surprises, at least on paper. It helps to weed out those with crim-inal histories, domestic violence charges, or those wanting to date when they're already married."

The audience laughed and Gwen nodded repeatedly.

"Yes, we definitely need *those* weeded out, don't we, ladies and gentlemen? Mm-hmm." Gwen turned to look at Marsali once more. "Marsali, you wrote a book on dating for good girls. Tell us a bit about that."

"I'd love to. I wrote the book when I was actively dating and realized the men I was meeting were mainly looking for hookups and not interested in something more substantial. I was frustrated and began to establish a set of rules or guidelines to use to weed them out. That became the catalyst for the book and ultimately the rules used by Marsali's Matches."

"What kinds of rules are we talking about here?"

"Well, the gentleman always pays for the first date. Always. It may seem sexist, but I found myself on a date once thinking my date would pay or at least split the check, but he had other ideas and I wound up paying the tab."

"Oh-ho! I'd say he didn't get a second date."

"He did not. Though he did ask," Marsali said, smiling. "Another rule is that my clients meet at the location and no home addresses or numbers are exchanged until at least the third date because usually by then you have a better idea of whether or not there's any crazy in the mix that the back-ground check didn't weed out."

Gwen laughed at the news. "What about all these people sending nudes? I take it that's a no-no, too?"

"Absolutely. If that's the kind of relationship you want, that's what you'll get. But if you're looking for something more, something that might potentially lead to the altar, you have to establish boundaries and see them through."

"I see. Well, I can understand that. I'm curious, though. You mentioned coming up with this when you were 'actively dating' and *I* think a matchmaker is only as good as good as her own perfect match. Am I right, audience? I mean, if she can't match herself, how can she accurately match others?"

The dig slid home and Marsali inwardly cringed. Why had she done this again? She felt her face begin to flush at the catcalls and whistles. "Um…"

"Now, now, Marsali. You *have* to give us the details. Your significant other has to be a gem of a man. I'm guessing tall, dark, and handsome?"

The audience response became even louder, and Marsali felt her entire body break out in sweat. Not the glistening kind but the kind that comes when fear takes hold. "Um… M-my perfect match… is, yes, I suppose he's all of those things."

"Oh? Go on."

Her brain scrambled like the eggs she'd tried to down this morning and couldn't due to nerves. She needed to end this topic. Now. "H-How about we discuss more of the suggestions included in my book?" Surely now the host would take a hint and change the subject?

"Oh, no, girl. You match people for a living. It's only fair you give us a name. Right?" Gwen said to the audience, waving at them to get their agreement. "You're too beautiful to be single. So who is your perfect man? Tell us, what's his name?"

Marsali wanted the floor to open up and swallow her. Was she really not going to be taken seriously because she wasn't attached? "I really can't—"

"*Of course* you can! We have to know who this perfect specimen of manhood is."

"Tell us!" a voice called from the audience.

"Does he have a brother?" asked another.

"Our viewing audience wants to know, girl-friend. Who is the matchmaker's secret?"

The crowd roared, the sound deafening.

This was it. The time to come clean and confess her single status. Her heart raced in her chest, pounding against her ribs, her palms sweaty and slick, the jacket too hot. "I'm not… I-I mean I—"

"Marsali, how can we believe in love when you won't share? You've already said he's tall, dark, and handsome. I'm guessing quite successful, too. Someone special you think of as your perfect match?"

"Oh, well. I-I do, but—"

"And his name is? Come on, sweet girl, we want details. You have to tell us or else how else can we believe in love?"

"Ollie," she blurted softly, and the microphone she wore picked up the breath of sound.

"Ahh, and there we have it," Gwen said, a sly grin forming on her face.

What? Had she really said it out loud? *No, no, no, no!*

"Girl, you should be shouting his name from the rooftops, not whispering," Gwen said. "Especially since Marsali's sweet *Ollie* is short for Hollywood hottie Oliver Beck."

The audience gasped collectively and erupted in applause, shouts, and whistles. The studio audience roared with deafening noise.

"Take a look at this. Our little hometown girl and Oliver Beck are *killing it*," Gwen said, "as you can see from this picture of the happy couple taken when Oliver was in Wilmington not long ago. How cute are they?"

Marsali looked around until she spotted the image being shown to the audience. The picture was zoomed in and showed her staring up at her brother's best friend with adoring eyes that revealed far too much for comfort. "I— How did you— That was a private gathering." Her parents' anniversary party, in fact.

"Oooh! Girl, we all know when it comes to Hollywood stars, ain't nothing private. Especially when they look like him! So tell us, Marsali, what is it like being Oliver Beck's girlfriend?"

Marsali stared into the blinding lights and stumbled through the next minute of live television looking like a fool with all of her ums, ahs, and silence when Gwen's questions bombarded her.

Obviously they'd kept things on the down low, so were they now going to take things to the next level? Was there a ring involved? Coming soon?

The very moment Gwen gave up trying to coerce another blundering response and the all clear was given, Marsali raced from the set to the ladies' room, gasping for breath when her phone began to ring. She ignored it but it kept ringing and ringing. She fumbled to silence it and groaned when she saw her brother's name appear above her mother's. Her father's. Her best friend, Eliza, who had boarded a cruise ship this morning for her honeymoon. A multitude of unknowns that were rapidly leaving voicemail messages. "Sweet baby Jesus," she said prayerfully, knowing only a higher power could ever deliver her from the mess she'd just created. "What have I done?"

Chapter 2

Oliver Beck watched the recorded interview end, all the while aware of his agent's impatient glare.

"You want to fill me in on anything? My phone is ringing off the hook with people wanting to know if Hollywood's hottest bachelor is off the market, and I'm looking like a fool because I don't know."

"I need to talk to Marsali."

"So it's *true*? I thought you were just friends? That she was some childhood hanger-on you haven't shaken loose yet."

Rikki leaned against the hotel's desk and crossed one ankle over the other. "You've been in Wilmington multiple times in the last year during filming, and again for her parents' anniversary party. Is that when you hooked up? Or was it before? Exactly how long have you been keeping this from me?"

Oliver found himself staring at his agent's ridiculous shoes, wondering how anyone could walk in six-inch heels, or better yet, why she'd wear them at all for a regular workday.

The sight made him appreciate Marsali's penchant for flip-flops and boat shoes whenever possible. "I need to talk to Marsali," he said again. He wasn't about to discuss his involvement with Marsali until he spoke with her and found out what was going on and why she hadn't immediately denied their dating status.

"Oliver, you are *the* most sought-after star right now, partly because you're good-looking and can actually act and partly because you're unattached. I have a *major* deal in the works, so if something has changed, I need to know so I can do damage control."

Damage control because he supposedly had a girlfriend? Seriously? Was his being single that important when it came to his career? "What deal?"

"I don't want to say just yet. But it's big. You don't want to do anything to screw this up, trust me."

His bodyguard shifted behind him and pulled

out his cell to glance at the face. The man was former Special Forces and built like a tank and now provided personal protection whenever Rikki felt Oliver needed it.

Oliver wondered if, at times, Rikki used the service as part of his image building, but whenever he was in a large city like New York for events, he'd admit the man earned his pay by keeping the more rabid fans at bay.

"Sir, your assistant just sent your itinerary," Denz said. "Ninety minutes to takeoff. We'll have to move if we're going to make it."

Oliver nodded in response and focused on Rikki. "Just keep me posted."

"Oliver, they want you for the lead male role. The script is on its way, and negotiations are already in progress. This is your next big move."

"I understand. I'll take a look at the script when I can, but right now I have a flight to catch."

"Back to California. Right?"

Oliver didn't answer and grabbed his backpack from the floor of the posh hotel room as he stood.

"Oliver," Rikki said. "You are going back to LA. Right? Your schedule is booked solid before the premiere."

"Actually I've been thinking of taking some time off."

"Now?"

"Why not?"

"Oh, I don't know, maybe because of everything I just said?"

"I can do the premiere interviews remotely."

"From where?"

"Does it matter?"

"Actually, it does. Where are you going? Are you seeing that woman?"

"That woman has a name."

"I don't care if she's the queen of England. Are you seriously involved with her?"

"Rikki, I have to go. I'll be in touch."

"Oliver! Oliver, stop!"

Oliver moved out of the hotel suite faster than Rikki could run after him in those heels of hers, and he and the bodyguard were on the elevator behind the sliding doors by the time she caught up.

Rikki's curse rang in his ears as the doors closed, and he knew he'd have to do something to make up for his rude departure, but right now his focus was getting to Marsali as quickly as possible.

"Would you like me to accompany you to Wilmington?" Denz asked.

Oliver looked at the burly guard and shook his head. "No. I should be fine. I'll touch base with you when I'm back in LA."

Denz cleared his throat and shifted his weight on his size-fourteen feet.

"Want me to do some background on Marsali Jones?"

Oliver smiled and shook his head at the idea of Marsali having a secret dark side. "No. I know her well, Denz. There's a good explanation for this, and I want to hear it in person."

"You'll let me know if something changes?"

"Yeah."

Denz accompanied Oliver through the hotel and out to a cab. They made it to the airport in record time.

Despite the urge to charter a jet to get to Wilmington faster, Oliver flew commercial. He'd made a promise to himself that no matter how weird or lucrative things got with his acting career, he wouldn't let it go to his head. Nor would he find himself broke if his career ended as quickly as it had begun ten years ago.

A former business major, he kept control of his money, did a regular review of his assets and investments, and made sure the people who worked for him weren't stealing from him.

Oliver flew first-class to get on and off quickly and for the extra leg room and did his best to keep a low profile with a hat and sunglasses. Traveling light helped since he didn't have to linger at baggage claim.

Once Oliver boarded, Denz would go to his gate to head to LAX.

Thankfully the flight to Wilmington, North Carolina, was uneventful and nonstop. Oliver pretended to sleep during the flight with his hat pulled low over his face and earbuds in place. Once off the aircraft, he moved through the crowd at ILM as fast as he could in an effort to not be recognized.

He hitched his fully loaded backpack higher on his shoulder and ducked his head as he dodged an out-of-control toddler. Wearing dark sunglasses inside the building might be a bit much, but he hoped he appeared as a hungover guy just trying to get home after a trip.

Outside, he quickly hailed a taxi, but as it drove toward him, Oliver heard a woman shriek.

"It's him! Oh, my gawd, it's Oliver Beck! It's *him*! He's here!"

So close.

The small crowd moving into and out of the airport turned in unison to stare where the woman pointed, and Oliver willed the taxi to pick up speed. People surged toward him right as the taxi stopped, and Oliver jumped inside and slammed the door, aware of the many cell phones pointed in his direction. "Go. Drive."

The taxi driver turned in the seat.

"You steal something? I ain't no getaway car."

"No. Please, just drive."

"Ah, man," the driver said, eyes widening. "You're that actor."

"Yeah, and I'll double your tip if you just get out of here."

"No worries, boss. I'm on it."

The crowd continued to record and a few young girls screamed as the taxi began to roll. Several of the braver ones banged on the taxi windows and proclaimed they loved him. One pressed her lips to the glass closest to him just as the taxi took off, and Oliver grimaced at the smear of lip gloss and grime on the window beside his head.

Finally they made it out from under the canopied area into the early-February sunshine. New York had been overcast and snowy, but Wilmington was a balmy fifty-six degrees. Cold due to the dampness of ocean and river, but warm with the sun.

"Where to, boss?"

Oliver quickly pulled the address up on his phone and relayed it to the driver.

"You here to see that girl? Does that mean it's true?"

He was already sick of hearing that question. Did everyone think his life was their business?

He grimaced at the question because he knew the answer. According to Rikki, privacy was the price to be paid and he had to deal with it. Ten years later, he was still trying to learn.

Oliver turned his face toward the dirty window and didn't respond to the driver's question.

That girl. Yeah, he was here to see Marsali. But this time was different. Thanks to her interview and what it had revealed.

The driver seemed to get that Oliver's lack of response was a response and stopped talking. They left the airport and moved through the city toward the south end of Wilmington and over the bridge to to Pleasure Island and the town of Carolina Cove.

Once they crossed the bridge, the taxi took Dow Road and picked up speed, closing the distance between him and his best friend's younger sister.

"Uh, boss? You sure you want me dropping you there? Looks like a hornet's nest compared to what happened at the airport."

Drawn from his thoughts, Oliver focused upon hearing the driver's words. The taxi slowed and Oliver peered out to see a small mob of reporters camped outside Marsali's house. So much for sneaking in quietly. "No. Keep driving. Take me a block over."

The driver kept going and made a turn onto the next street. Oliver hoped he wouldn't have the cops after him if her neighbors saw him skulking about. That is, if he recognized her house from the back. He should've paid closer attention, but when Marsali was around, he wasn't focused on the surroundings.

Oliver paid the driver and got out, shouldering his backpack. Marsali lived in a quiet neighborhood of older homes, most with fenced yards. Dressed as he was in hat and sunglasses, with his bag, he'd probably get pegged as an intruder. His agent wouldn't appreciate him getting shot, but then Rikki didn't appreciate anything that might damage the goods she worked so hard to peddle.

Oliver turned to face the house he guessed was behind Marsali's being that it was midway down the street like hers. An older man was outside getting his mail. He eyed Oliver's exit from the taxi and watched as Oliver approached. "Excuse me, sir. Beautiful day, isn't it?"

"I don't want any."

Oliver laughed. "I'm not selling anything, sir. I believe my taxi let me out on the wrong street. I'm trying to get to Seashell Lane. Would it be okay if I cut through your yard?"

The man eyed him once again, and because Oliver felt the man trying to get a gauge on him, Oliver removed his sunglasses and wished he'd taken the time to get a haircut and shave before boarding the flight from New York City. Maybe then he wouldn't look so shaggy.

"I suppose it would be all right if you did."

"Thank you, sir."

The older man led the way to the gate at the side of his garage and opened it, holding it for Oliver to walk through before shutting it behind him.

"You know, I know the neighbor behind me," the man said casually as they crossed the yard in the back. "She brought me meals when she found out my wife had cancer."

That sounded like something Marsali would do,

and Oliver hoped it meant he'd guessed correctly. "That's nice."

"Saw her on the local news last night and this morning. Saw you, too."

Oliver winced at the man's statement, but at least it confirmed his navigation skills. "I see. I'm, uh, sorry for misleading you, sir, but her house has reporters out front."

"Yup. Been there all day. Spotted them when I went to the store early this morning. Son, Marsali's a nice girl and a good neighbor. I wouldn't think much of a man who'd take advantage of that goodness."

"I understand, sir."

"I suppose what I'm asking is if you plan on breaking that sweet girl's heart?"

Oliver felt the words like a punch to the gut and shook his head. "I'm hoping she won't break mine, sir. I've known Marsali a long time. Sixteen years," he added when the man looked skeptical. "Her brother is my best friend and Marsali… I'd never do anything to deliberately hurt her."

"Well, I suppose that's fair." The old man opened the back gate. "I'll leave this unlocked. In case you find yourself needing a way out undetected."

Oliver held out his hand and shook the old man's. "Thank you, sir. I appreciate it."

The old man nodded.

"One of her lasagnas wouldn't go unappreciated, either."

Oliver chuckled. "I'll relay that message—I'm sorry, I didn't ask your name."

"Paul."

"Paul. I appreciate your help. I'm Oliver but… I suppose you already knew that."

"You'll have to jump her fence. She doesn't have a back gate, only one on the front side, where those reporters could see you. Might want to watch out for her dog, too."

"Dog?" When had she gotten a dog? It hadn't been that long since he'd talked to her.

Paul grinned. "You can run fast, right?"

Oliver wasn't sure if the man was teasing him or not, but Oliver squeezed through the tight opening of the fence abutting Marsali's and eyed her elegant black metal one, thankful it was only about four feet high. He tossed his backpack over the top and swung himself up and over.

Paul watched from his property while Oliver picked up his bag and quickly made his way across Marsali's backyard and patio to her door. He knocked and heard barking on the other side. Apparently Paul hadn't lied about the dog.

"I said no comment. Go away!" Marsali called from inside.

Oliver lifted his hand and knocked again, rapping the coded knock he and Marsali's brother had used in college when they'd come to Mac and Marsali's parents' house on long weekends. The knock was to alert Marsali when Mac and Oliver needed her to let them inside after a night out on the town.

"Mac?"

"No." Oliver waited, staring hard at the door's curtained window. After a long pause, he saw the curtain move and Marsali's beautiful freckled face appeared, eyes wide as saucers. "Let me in."

She blinked and he could almost see the wheels cranking in her brain as to whether or not that was a good idea.

"I'm *sorry*, Ollie. Really, I am."

Her words were muffled through the glass but emotionally charged and full of regret. Did that mean she *didn't* mean to say what she had? "Let me in, Marsali."

"Are you terribly angry?"

"Open the door and find out."

The curtain fluttered back into place, and several more seconds went by while the barking continued. Finally a click sounded and the door opened. Oliver slipped his foot inside before she could change her mind and entered her home, watching as she grabbed her dog by its harness.

"I can't believe you came all the way here. How did you get in my backyard?"

"Your neighbor, Paul. He'd like a lasagna, by the way."

A near-hysterical laugh bubbled out of her chest. She turned to face him, all wild brown curls that could never quite be tamed. Marsali had that beach-girl-next-door look about her. The curls and freckles and year-round tan. There was just something about Carolina girls... Especially this one.

"Ollie, I am so, *so* sorry. I didn't mean for this to happen. Your name just slipped out and then I couldn't take it back and she had that photo and everyone was yelling and things got out of control before I could even—"

"When did you get a dog?" he asked, interrupting her rambling. He eyed the oversized puppy that appeared to be a golden retriever mix.

"What? Oh, um, she's a foster. I've only had her a week," she said as she took the puppy toward a wire kennel. "Ginger is afraid of people and gets snippy."

"Let me see her."

"Really? You want a dog bite on top of everything I've already done to you?"

The dog began growling as Marsali carried it closer to Oliver, but once Marsali stood within reach, Oliver slowly lifted his hand for the dog to take a few cautious sniffs. That done, he opened his fingers and lightly ran them over the dog's head. "You named her Ginger from *Gilligan's Island*," he said, smiling. "You are seriously obsessed with that show."

Marsali lifted her shoulder in a shrug, still not making eye contact.

"She needed a name. And I like clean comedy."

That was something he admired about her. Marsali lived a sheltered life. The sweet kind that made him think of old TV reruns and a time when the world wasn't as crazy and debauched as it was today. It might seem unrealistic to some, but he found her choices and sweetness appealing.

"Ollie, will you please forgive me? I've ruined our lives but I swear it wasn't on purpose."

Oliver dumped his bag on the couch while Marsali lowered Ginger to the floor. Oliver waited for her to straighten and lifted his hands to Marsali's upper arms and gently gripped, then pulled her against his chest for a hug like he had a hundred times before over the years. "Breathe."

She stilled for a moment then inhaled shakily.

"There you go," he murmured, running his hands up her tense back. "Hi."

"Hi."

"It's going to be fine."

"Nothing about this mess is *fine*."

"It will be." She gave a very unladylike snort she probably wouldn't recommend for the female clients of Marsali's Matches, and smiled. "I have to ask you something, though."

"What?"

The word came out muffled because she'd pressed her face into his chest. "Why me? When the reporter asked for a name, you could've said any name, but you said mine."

"I-I— It just came out."

"Mm. I'm pretty sure you know a lot of single men. Especially with that database of yours," he said, not allowing himself to think too long on the fact that she went to mixers and networking events all over the country to recruit new clients too busy to date on their own.

He didn't doubt most of the men agreed to sign up because it meant talking to Marsali and getting some one-on-one time during their personal interview that they hoped would turn into more. "Why not name one of them?"

"I know I should have but when she was describing who… You came to mind and your name came out. I didn't mean for it to."

"Marsali, I believe the host's words—your words —were *perfect match*. You think of me that way?" he asked.

He felt Marsali stiffen, and she broke the embrace and started backstepping away from him.

"It just happened so fast. I'm sorry, Ollie. I'll fix it. I will. I just need time to gather my thoughts and prepare a statement. Your Hollywood hunk status will not be in danger any longer than necessary."

"You didn't answer my question."

"Ollie, come on. It's obvious you'd make s-some woman a good match. You know that."

"So why didn't you set Gwen straight on the air when you had the chance?"

"I should've. And I know right now you're either highly amused or ticked off or b-both," she said, "but it was an innocent slip of the tongue."

"Are you sure about that?" He matched her

steps, closing the distance between them once more with his longer stride.

Her back hit the dining room wall behind her, and her eyes widened when he braced his forearm by her head, letting his fingers tangle in her wild mane of curls atop her head. He held her gaze, letting her see everything he'd held in check for sixteen agonizing years. "You're sure that's all it was?"

Her full lips parted to drag in a ragged breath, and he fought back the urge to kiss her like he'd wanted to for so long.

"Wh-what?"

She had the most amazing eyes he'd ever seen. They were a mix of golden brown and forest green swirled together and surrounded by dark blue. No one had eyes like her. They were as unique as she was, and he'd often found himself drowning in the depths. Like now. "Are you sure that's all it was? A slip"—he let his gaze lower to her mouth, just as drawn by her full lips—"of the tongue?"

Chapter 3

Marsali felt the intensity of Oliver's stare like a physical caress. "*Stop* messing with me," she said, an uncomfortable laugh bubbling out of her chest. Her heart pounded hard and she fought back the seemingly ever-present flush of heat she felt whenever he was around.

Now having him look at her the way he was, stand so close… Gah, he gave a girl a head rush just from being near him, and when he turned on that Hollywood sexiest-man stuff, her insides melted to goo.

But she knew it was all a show. A performance. Because the one thing she and Oliver Beck weren't was *that*.

Ollie smiled that beautiful smile that had

captured the attention of the modeling company and launched his rising star after they'd spotted a photo of him online soaked to the skin. Oliver had jumped into the Intercoastal to save two puppies that had fallen off of a dock. Between the heart-wrenching photo, his shredded build, and that blinding smile, he'd skyrocketed into fame, moving from modeling into acting in the blink of an eye. He was considered a natural, full of charm and charisma. A man's man and a woman's dream.

Right now Oliver's famous smile sent a bolt of heat zapping through her body, bringing tingles and sparks and awareness that only Ollie could create.

Oh, she'd had a crush on him as a teenager, sure. What girl wouldn't have? But she'd grown out of it.

At least, she thought she had until that televised blunder.

Freudian slip?

It had to be.

"Why do you think I'm messing with you?"

"Oh, get real. You've always messed with me, teased me. And I know I deserve whatever revenge you dish out after the trouble I've caused you, but please… Now is not the time. I have to think."

"Fine," he said, taking a step back. "Revenge can wait."

She inhaled a ragged breath now that she actually *could* breathe again and hoped he couldn't tell how shaky it sounded.

She and Oliver were friends, had always been friends, would only be friends, because that's the way they worked. He was… her second big brother. And even she knew it would be twisted to feel *that* way about someone she considered *brotherly*, if only because it helped her keep her mind off things she shouldn't be thinking.

"But remember you started it."

Her uncomfortable laugh turned into a groan. "Trust me, I am well aware of that mistake. And I will fix it—as soon as I get my nerve up to face the group out front."

"Have you talked to your parents?"

Marsali winced and shook her head. "No. I was so mortified I've avoided them. I was going to call you and try to explain but… here you are."

"You can only avoid people for so long, Marsali. Those reporters aren't going away anytime soon."

"I know. I've been working on a statement but… I can't find the words," she said, motioning toward the desk just off of the kitchen, surrounded by her dozen or so attempts wadded up on the floor because she'd missed the trash bin more often than not.

Oliver moved across her house with the ease of a man confident in his own skin and made himself comfortable on the floor near Ginger. The puppy stopped playing and stared at Ollie as though unsure of whether he could be trusted, but the dog cautiously moved toward Oliver after a moment.

Marsali watched as Oliver gave Ginger the time she needed to get comfortable before lifting a finger to initiate contact. Once the puppy deemed that okay, Oliver added a few more fingers until he was able to pet the dog without her rearing back and scrambling away in fear. The man was irresistible, even to people-wary dogs.

"What's her story?"

"Dog hoarder that was probably a fighter. She was one of forty-seven dogs taken from a home. Ollie, why did you come? I mean, I'm glad you're here. You're always welcome. But why not just call? Are you that angry with me?"

He looked up at her from his prone position on the floor, and once more she was treated to a smile. The man seriously didn't know how dangerous he was to females. Or maybe he did? How could he not know after all these years and the success he'd had?

Since he'd been discovered by Hollywood, they'd spent less time together in person. Short visits here and there every year, with Mac and her parents around. They were rarely alone, though they did text quite often. Ollie would share news of his travels and pics of film stars he knew she liked, ask about her day, and she would tell him funny stories about her clients.

"I wanted to check on you. In person. It's not easy dealing with that kind of media."

"You've got that right."

"What did Mac have to say?"

She silently groaned at the thought of her brother's reaction. She'd avoided *all* calls last night.

Thankfully Mac was out of town on business, and her parents were now snowbirds who stayed in Florida over the winter months, but she knew it was only a matter of time before she could no longer hide from the inevitable. "I haven't talked to him yet either. I needed time to recover from my embarrassment. I'll come up with a statement or post a video telling everyone it was a misunderstanding and we're just friends. I *will*, I just…"

"You just what?"

Was she a horrible person? She had to be to be so selfish. "Dread the fallout. Since that aired, my part-time assistant said she's scheduled three months' worth of interviews for potential clients, and my editor called and left a message stating that they definitely want my idea for another book on navigating relationships in the modern age. Once I tell them the truth…"

"All that could disappear."

"Yup. My credibility will be ruined. Yay, me."

"So, don't tell them."

She shifted her gaze back to him and found Oliver staring at her. "What?"

"You could do what you said, issue a statement and such. But there is an alternative."

Marsali wondered if she'd heard him correctly. Because surely he hadn't just said—and in his actor's bedroom voice no less— "An alternative?"

After the disaster of an interview last evening, she'd come home and shuttered her windows, drowning her embarrassment in a half bottle of wine and snuggle time with Ginger. This morning she'd woken up to a headache, a mob of reporters out front, and no other choices.

"Marsali?"

She startled at Oliver's voice and forced herself

to focus. Now was not the time for her brain to be wandering off into La-La Land. "You didn't have to fly coast-to-coast, Ollie."

He looked confused by the change in topic.

"I wasn't on the West Coast. I was in New York and heading back to Cali when my agent appeared at my hotel wanting answers about my girlfriend status. Don't say you're sorry again," he said when she opened her mouth to do just that. "I'm here because I want to be. I'm… curious."

Curious? "I've embarrassed us both and ruined our lives."

"Hardly."

He slowly shoved himself upright and got to his feet in a graceful surge, moving toward her with his long-legged stride. She realized then the movie companies did that a lot, filmed Ollie walking, running, moving. Probably because he looked so *good doing it.*

Focus, for pity's sake.

He stopped in front of her and took her hands in his.

"This isn't the end of the world, you know."

"Not for you. You'll be fine. You're *you* whereas I'm the crazy woman who dropped your name in an interview on a show that hindsight says I shouldn't have been on in the first place, because *un*like you, I don't have an agent to guide me, and now I won't ever need one. Oh, Ollie, how could I be so stupid? Why did I go? I *knew* better than to—"

"Breathe, Marsali."

"I can't! Because even though it was a-an honest mistake, who's going to believe me? Huh? They'll think I tried to use your name to get attention and ride your coattails. That I'm a-a gold digger of a friend. I'm *ruined*," she said, the words ending on a groan as she yanked her hands from his so she could bury her face in her palms before raking her fingers through her mop of unruly hair. "My credibility as a dating coach. My business as a matchmaker. The future book deal? Gwen was right. A single matchmaker *doesn't* make a good impression, which is something my editor *has* said to me before, but to panic like that and-and… Once the truth is out, *no one* is going to want to hire me *or* read my book. I'm a joke, and I have no one to blame but myself."

"You done yet?"

She glared at him and wondered if she was going to become one of those people who day drank on a regular basis. "I'm allowed to vent some, aren't I?"

Oliver took hold of her elbows and ran his hands lightly up and down her arms in a soothing gesture. The problem was it brought her even closer to him, and she remembered a scene from one of his movies when he'd rolled over in bed and the sheet had ridden low over his taut abs and—

"You're blushing. What are you thinking about?"

She blinked to awareness and gaped up at him, fully dressed and scruffy and standing in her living room mere feet from the crumpled apology attempt she'd yet to finish writing. "I'm wondering what I'm going to do for a living now that my life is over."

"Come here."

He wrapped his arms around her and squeezed her tight and she welcomed the embrace. The studies on anxiety and the benefits of hugs were dead accurate. Until the hug ended and the world swallowed her up again with its cold, harsh reality of no clients, no book advance, and a mortgage she wouldn't be able to pay.

Was she really going to be that thirty-year-old woman having to move back home to live with her parents?

"Look," he said softly, "I get that you're freaked out. But the sooner you finish the spiral, the sooner we can talk about a solution."

"What solution? You mean me owning up to the fact my business is done for? Obviously I'm not ready to face that or I'd be on my porch already, giving the statement I haven't been able to write."

"Who says it has to be that way?"

"How can it be any *other* way? You know what's going to happen. I'm not exaggerating."

"Maybe not. Unless… we give them what they want."

She lifted her head and bumped his chin in the process. "What?"

"Marsali," he said, his tone growing a tad impatient sounding. "Focus."

"I'm trying. I'm just a little preoccupied by my career-ending faux pas."

"I can see where telling them the truth would cause you difficulty, but pull yourself together and listen to me."

"You don't think I did this on purpose, do you, Ollie?"

He smoothed his hand up her back to her neck and gently rubbed the tension he found. Marsali held her breath to smother the moan of pleasure that begged to erupt. Her whole body was one tight rubber band ready to snap.

"You know, you are the only one who's ever called me that."

"Because"—she struggled to keep her voice level—"I knew you hated it and it was the only way I could get you to look at me back then. Consider it insult to injury now, I guess," she said. "Even though it's habit."

"I did plenty of looking, trust me. And I made you think I hated it, but I actually didn't mind so long as you were the only one."

She leaned more heavily against him and treasured the moment. Typical Oliver. He really was a nice guy. Which was why his name had come to mind when the host had asked the question, but *why* had she said it out loud? She mentally kicked herself for the millionth time.

"Marsali?"

"Hmm?"

"Fixing this isn't as hard as you think."

"How's that?" she asked, lifting her head from where she rested it against his broad chest. "Because from where I'm standing, it only ends one way and that's badly."

"That's if you admit we're not dating. But what if we were?"

She used her arms to push away from him, not

only to get some much-needed breathing room from the drug-like haze she'd fallen into being cradled in his arms but to stare up at him as well. "Come again?"

"What if we do exactly what that host and fans think we've *been* doing?"

"Date?"

"Why not? The world apparently likes it given the press and your upswing in clients, so let's make it real. Date me."

Marsali stared at Oliver, getting the full Hollywood treatment of sexy-mussed hair, jaw scruff, and piercing dark eyes that left her weak-kneed. Did he have to smell so good? Look so good? *Feel* so strong and hard and dependable? "You're kidding, right?" she asked, torn between horror and disbelief.

"No."

"It's not that I don't… It's just… Ollie, you don't have to do this."

"What, exactly, do you think I'm doing?"

"*Pity*-dating me so I don't look like such a fool. I'm grateful that you're willing. Don't get me wrong. But it's too much to ask of you."

"You're not asking. I'm offering."

"*Why?*"

"If the situation was reversed, you'd do the same for me. Don't tell me you wouldn't."

She opened her mouth to argue but it was true. Still… what woman wanted to land a relationship that way? Even a fake one?

"Look, Marsali, maybe you said my name by mistake and things were taken out of context, but you said it, and I'd like to think at least part of your reasoning is because you trust me. Because you know I'd never let anything hurt you."

"Yeah, but—"

"No buts. If we date, the problem is solved."

"Not when Mac kills us both."

"You'd rather face the reporters instead of your brother?"

She fisted her hands and battled the barrage of questions and doubts and thoughts pummeling her. "No. But Mac would have to be dealt with. And then there's my parents and your agent and people like my assistant and Eliza—"

"The fewer people who know it's pretend, the better."

"You mean not tell them? Mac would hate us. Because of that interview, he probably believes we've been dating behind his back."

"I know. But the more people who know the

truth, the more likely it is that this plan won't work. Someone will slip up and reveal something they shouldn't."

She hated that her actions had brought them both to this point. To lying and deceiving. To her family. His friends. "I don't know, Ollie…"

"What's holding you back?"

"You mean beyond lying to people I love? Maybe why you would even consider this? What do you get out of it?"

He rested his forearms on her shoulders and she liked the weight of them. It made her feel grounded in a sense. Connected. As fast as her heart pounded in her chest and her thoughts raced, it helped.

"I get to be the hero for you in this scenario and I like that. You need me, and I want to help. We'll figure out the details as we go along, but for now all that matters is that we show everyone, including the press, a united front."

The man before her wasn't Oliver Beck, movie star. He was Ollie, her Ollie, who'd made Mac hold a funeral when her pet gerbil died and who'd blackened Peter Sanders's eye when he'd started a rumor about her after her senior prom.

Now as she stared into Oliver's eyes, Marsali felt like she teetered on a cliff, one step away from the biggest free fall of her life. But what choice did she have after the mess she'd made of things? "You really want to do this?"

"Yes."

Because that was Ollie. "I confess I'd rather eat mud pies than go out there and tell them I blundered my way into this mess because I was too embarrassed to say I was single."

"Agree to the plan, and you won't have to."

"I don't... I don't know what to say."

He flashed his famous Hollywood smile—the one she'd known six glorious years before Hollywood came knocking—and her heart pounded hard in her chest.

"Say yes. Marsali Jones," he said, his voice changing to a formal tone, "will you do me the honor of dating me?"

Chapter 4

Oliver waited for Marsali's response and wondered if he'd pushed too hard.

Of course he had. He should've waited to see if Marsali suggested the idea and gone along with it. But he wasn't willing to risk her *not* bringing it up so…

"Yes. I mean, if you seriously don't mind pretending?"

"I don't mind at all."

"Just until I can get some of the new clients happily matched so they don't go running the moment they realize we aren't together, and I get the first few chapters to my editor so she sees what a great idea it *really* is, and—"

"You got it."

"You're sure?"

"Yes."

"Oh! Ollie, thank you! Thank you, thank you, thank you," she cried, surging toward him and wrapping him in a huge hug.

He welcomed the weight of her once again but this time lifted her off of her feet, her laughter hot and heady in his ear. After a long moment, he set her back down, but when she started to pull away, he didn't release her.

"Ollie?"

He ignored the flare of panic in her eyes and lowered his head toward hers. "Pretending will only get us so far. Dating couples kiss, Marsali. Which means we need to practice."

"N-now?"

"Our first time can't be in front of cameras with analysts trying to decode our body language by watching our every move." He brushed his thumb over her lower lip.

"Um…"

He closed the distance and brushed his lips over hers, capturing the sound. He didn't rush the moment but kept things light, knowing there would be more kisses later. Many, many more. For now he was content so long as he got this, their first but not the last. He wanted her taste, her scent. Everything Marsali.

She kissed like an angel, hesitant, allowing him to take the lead while luring him in with her taste. The softness of her full lips had haunted him for far too many years, and this was the reward for his patience as he tasted sweet tea and chocolate and something mysterious, indefinably her.

Marsali ended the kiss and pulled away from him, avoiding his gaze. Her cheeks were flushed to a rosy hue and her heavy-lidded gaze told him what he needed to know. What she didn't say. She was as intrigued and drawn to him as he was to her, and he thanked God for the discernment.

"Ollie… I'm sorry. I-I don't think I can agree to this plan of yours."

"Marsali—"

She pushed him away and took several steps back, her tongue flicking over her lips.

"There has to be another way besides us acting like something we're not."

"You didn't like kissing me?"

She wouldn't look him in the eyes.

"It's… Even if I was okay with pretending for a while, we didn't think this through."

"How so?"

"My family *knows* we haven't been dating."

"Do you tell them every detail of your life?"

"No, of course not, but—"

"Then they couldn't know with one hundred percent certainty."

"Okay, the press and your fans then. They won't believe it."

"Why do you think that?"

"Because you date models and movie stars. Don't give me that look. You know exactly what I mean. Your usual arm candy never eats and they go for spa days where they're lasered and injected and look like sex on a stick."

Sex on a stick? He couldn't help but chuckle at the description considering most of them couldn't form a coherent sentence that wasn't riddled with drama, much less run a successful company and write books. "You do realize you're an insanely talented, beautiful woman, right?"

Her phone began ringing again and she stared at him for a long moment before she groaned and hurried across the room.

It was in those seconds following his question that he realized she had no clue how beautiful she was. Maybe not as the model-actress type, but

Marsali was a natural beauty with her freckles and softness and curves.

"Great," she said, staring at her phone. "It's Mac calling again. I have to call him and my parents back soon or they're going to call an intervention."

"I'll handle it."

"What? No, I'm to blame for all of this. I just don't know what to say."

Oliver took his cell from his pocket and unlocked his screen to find six calls from Mac. "You're not the only one he's contacted." He pressed the call button.

"What are you doing? Ollie, no!"

"What is going on with you and my sister?"

Oliver winced at Mac's shout and held the phone away from his ear, all the while watching the color drain from Marsali's face when her brother's angry voice carried across the room. "Mac, calm down."

"Calm do— seriously? Where are you?" Mac demanded.

Oliver heard a car door slam outside and moved across her living room toward the front of the house to get a look.

Mac was striding up to the front door with the

phone pressed to his ear and the reporters practically tripping over themselves to get a shot of the action even though it was just of Mac's back.

Oliver turned to see Marsali standing nearby and frowned. He needed a firm commitment from her to move forward with the plan before her brother arrived to talk her out of it.

"Marsali, it's me," Mac called, knocking. "And just so you know," Mac said into the phone, "there's a slew of reporters outside her place just waiting to take a bite out of her. You need to do something about this, Oliver."

Without a word, Oliver stepped behind the panel so he was out of view of the reporters Mac complained about and unlocked the door. Mac quickly stepped inside and shut it behind him. "Oliver, you—"

"Hey," Oliver said.

Mac's eyes widened just a tad before he calmly lowered the phone from his ear and slipped it into his rear pocket. That done, he grabbed Oliver by the shirt and pinned him up against the closest wall.

"Mac, no!" Marsali cried, rushing toward them.

"You stay out of this," Mac said, drawing his arm back to take a swing.

Marsali squeezed between them just as Mac let

the fist fly, and despite trying to shield her, Mac's fist bounced off of Oliver's forearm into Marsali's face.

"Oh!"

Mac took a step back, visibly horrified by what had happened, while Oliver quickly tucked Marsali behind him and examined her. "Are you all right? Let me see. Put your hands down and—"

"I'm fine."

"Let me see."

"Get your hands off of her. She said she's fine," Mac ordered.

Oliver gently lifted her chin from her chest and brushed her hands away from her mouth, noting the slight redness at the corner. "I don't think that's going to bruise but we'd best get you some ice."

"Marse, I'm sorry. I am, but *you* can get ice while I talk to Oliver."

"I'm not leaving you two alone," Marsali said. "Not when that's how you behave."

"I didn't mean to hit you."

"No, you meant to hit him and that's not okay," she said. "If you want to be mad, be mad at me because *I'm* the reason this is happening."

"What's not okay is this Hollywood playboy messing around with my baby sister."

Hollywood playboy?

"Ice that before you look like a bad lip job," Mac ordered.

Rolling her eyes at them, Marsali stomped off toward the kitchen. Oliver followed her, because if he and Mac were going to battle it out, they needed to be as far away from the reporters as possible.

"Oliver, we had a deal."

"A deal? What kind of deal?" Marsali asked, frowning as she quickly wrapped an ice cube in a towel and held it to her mouth.

"That Oliver would never try anything with you. *Ever*. Remember?" Mac demanded, glaring at Oliver. "How long has this been going on? How long have the two of you been sneaking around?"

"Mac, please, don't be like that," Marsali said, her expression one of regret. "This isn't what you think. Ollie and I—"

"Never meant to hurt you," Oliver said, cutting Marsali off before she could reveal their plan.

Mac folded his arms over his chest and split his attention between the two of them.

"One of you had better start talking. Fast."

"Marsali slipped when she said my name but it's time for the truth to come out."

"Over my dead body," Mac said. "You promised me you'd keep your hands off of my sister."

"Mac... Ollie. Stop!"

"If she goes out there and tells them we aren't dating, her credibility is shot. Her career, her book deal, is over in a two-minute news clip," Oliver said to Mac. "It'll ruin her."

"You have a new book deal?" Mac asked.

"Possibly. It… depends."

"On you dating him?" Mac said with a wave of his hand in Oliver's direction.

"Considering my editor called after the interview aired, yeah."

"Ah, Marse. How could you let this happen? How could *you?*" Mac demanded of Oliver.

Oliver winced. Death by best friend wasn't the way he wanted to go out of this world.

"Mac, I-I…" Marsali looked from her brother to Oliver, and he could read the indecision on her features. Marsali was torn and wanted to tell her brother the truth but fear held her back.

She wasn't deceptive by nature, and while Oliver didn't like the thought of lying to anyone, especially Mac, he knew the risk involved should anyone else know the truth. He also wouldn't allow himself to consider the fact he hoped to change their dating status for real, because that was an obstacle to tackle one step at a time.

Oliver walked over to where she stood and put his arm around Marsali's shoulders, drawing her to his side.

"Get your hands off of her."

"Stop fighting," Marsali said. "You're *best friends*."

"Not anymore. That ended when you started acting like one of his fan-girls."

Marsali gasped at the insult, and Oliver quickly inserted himself between the siblings when Marsali charged toward her much bigger older brother.

"You," she said, pointing at Mac, "had better keep those kinds of comments to yourself or I'll be the one bloodying *your* lip!"

"I'm sorry about that, but it wouldn't have happened if you hadn't jumped in between us," Mac said.

"You shouldn't have tried to hit him!"

"Marsali, you're in over your head. What were you thinking, letting this happen? Mom and Dad are beside themselves with worry."

Oliver flinched at the news. He'd always gotten along well with Marsali's parents, but then as a friend of Mac's, why wouldn't he? Apparently now things were different, though, because otherwise they'd be happy at the thought of their daughter dating him. "Mac, I know you're having a hard time accepting this but don't disrespect Marsali."

"A hard time? Yeah, I'm having a hard time. Marse, it's not too late. Go out there and… I don't know, tell them you used to date but you broke up," Mac ordered. "Tell them it's *over*. Say that photo circulating on the internet is just of two friends. End this mess before it gets crazier than it already is and you wind up getting hurt."

Marsali looked up at Oliver, and he could read the indecision and doubt in her eyes. Maybe he should let her off the hook. Mac's idea could be enough to help her salvage her career.

It would be simpler.

Probably safer.

She'd get the benefit of his name and the free press and save face when it came to her book and matchmaking service. "They'll see right through that," he said instead. "Know it's a lie."

He pushed the limits with that statement, but he wasn't going to willingly give up what might be his only chance to date Marsali like he'd always wanted.

She inhaled and sighed and once more he found her leaning against him. This time it was of her own accord and he welcomed the weight of her and the awareness that it came out of trust.

She trembled against him and he hated the toll this was having on her. Stress was never a good thing.

"Mac, I can't do that."

A low curse came from the other side of the room before Mac stalked toward the front door and slammed out of the house.

Oliver pulled Marsali close and cradled her against his chest, breathing in the coconut scent of her hair.

"I'm sorry," she whispered.

"For what?"

"Coming between you and Mac. He isn't going to forgive this easily."

Oliver tightened his hold on her. "He'll get over it eventually. It's fine."

"It's not fine. If you were smart, you'd go back to California."

"It would be hard to date you from there."

"I'm still not sure this is wise."

"If you're hesitant because of Mac, don't worry. We'll sort it out."

"You're going to get tired of Mac and my family hating on you, and of the hassle I've brought into your life. You're going to wonder why you ever agreed to do this in the first place. Maybe it *would* be better if we said it was over."

He tucked his hand under her chin and lifted it so he could see her beautiful eyes, so full of worry and regret and apprehension. "Either way, I'm not leaving you to face it alone."

Oliver lowered his head and sealed the promise with a kiss that left blood rushing through his veins as her fingers tightened on his arms, her short nails digging lightly into his skin. He kept things light and easy, careful of the bruise at the corner of her mouth.

She ended the "practice" kiss far too soon for his liking, and he realized she'd heard the cell phone ringing from the kitchen counter whereas he'd tuned it out.

"That's my parents. Again."

Her voice sounded low and raspy and everything he'd dreamed it would be after a moment like they'd just shared. He pressed another kiss to her full lips before releasing her and backing up a step. He liked that her cheeks were filled with hot color, eyes dark. She wasn't as unmoved by the kiss as she tried to appear. "Are you going to answer it?"

She'd stood there staring at him as though

unable to decide, and he liked that he got to her. She got to him, too.

Marsali snatched the phone off the charge cord and swiped a finger across the screen.

"Mama, hang on a sec."

She kept going toward the hallway and the half bath beyond. "Marsali," Oliver called after her, "keeping the plan secret is the only way it will work."

He watched as her shoulders sank as she shut the door.

Chapter 5

Marsali propped herself on the closed lid of the toilet and took a fortifying breath before lifting the phone to her ear. "Hi, Mama."

"Marsali! Honey, *what* is going on? Your brother called and said— Well, I'm not sure I understood what he said, he was talking so fast, but he confirmed that you and Oliver are *dating*? When did this happen? Why haven't you said anything?"

"It's… complicated, Mama. I'm sorry. I-I should've called you back last night but things have been… Well, things have been crazy."

"Mac said Oliver is there right now?"

Marsali winced. "Yes, he is."

"Marsali, honey, you know we love you and

respect you, but are you sure about a relationship with him?"

"Um."

"I mean, there's the coast-to-coast distance and his fame… the women who *throw themselves* at him. You've seen the videos of his appearances. Oliver is a wonderful man, but that's a lot of stress on top of regular relationship conflicts."

"Mama, I… I really don't want to talk about it right now, okay? I just wanted to answer and say I'm okay and I'll… talk to you later. Maybe tonight. Or tomorrow."

"Marsali, are you okay? You don't sound like yourself."

Her mother had always been able to read her tone like a psychic with a working crystal ball. The kind of insight that came from too many years as a psychologist, no doubt. "I'm fine. I'm just tired. I didn't sleep well last night."

"I imagine it wasn't easy having your relationship become public as it did."

"No. Mama—"

"I know, you have to go. But know I'm here if you want to talk. Always. And just so you're aware, there are a couple of reporters here, too."

Oh, no. "Don't talk to them. Please. Oliver and I will… We'll make a statement or something soon."

"Okay. We won't."

"I love you," Marsali said, wondering why she didn't just tell her mother the truth and get it over with. Of all people, her mother would probably be the most understanding of how things had gotten out of hand.

But then, her mother would also have to comment on the reasons why Marsali had publicly named Oliver and that… that was something Marsali wasn't ready to delve into just yet. In this instance, the less her parents knew, the better, because either way, they'd worry the way parents did.

"I love you, too."

Marsali said goodbye and ended the call but remained in the bathroom. She needed to make a firm decision. Was she really going to go through with Ollie's plan?

Do you want to be able to pay your bills?

She hurried to open an app on her phone and clicked on Eliza's name. *I'm okay. Insane but okay. Can't give details but I'll explain when you get back from your cruise. Enjoy and don't worry! HAVE FUN!*

There. Maybe that would at least keep Eliza

from jumping ship the first chance she could just to find out what was going on instead of enjoying her honeymoon. The last thing Marsali wanted to do was ruin it.

A soft knock at the door drew her attention.

"Marsali, you okay in there?" Oliver asked.

"Yeah."

"You coming out?"

"Do I have to?"

She heard Oliver's low, sexy chuckle through the door.

"How about you go get ready and we'll head out for lunch somewhere."

She froze, the phone biting in her hand where she gripped it so hard. "You want to go out there?"

"Marsali, open the door."

She rolled her eyes at his insistence on face-to-face conversation but did as ordered. Once the door was opened, Oliver took a step back.

"Did you tell your parents the truth?"

"No."

"Why didn't you?"

She stopped when he braced an arm against the wall, blocking her way to the living room.

"I don't know. I just... couldn't. I didn't want

them to think badly of me for cracking under pressure."

"That wouldn't happen."

"Yeah, well, I'm not so sure. They're both very successful in their fields. They give talks and lectures and interviews. I don't recall either one of them panicking on television."

"Anyone in your shoes might've done the same thing. The host seemed pretty good at stirring up drama."

"You can say that again. But I bet you would've kept your cool. I saw your last interview. When the host asked if you were single or taken or what, you just smiled and let them wonder. Why didn't *I* do that? Why do people think if you're unattached, you can't be good at doing what I do?"

"I don't know. But we're going to make this okay."

"Lying is not okay, but I can't bring myself to face them now."

"You don't have to. And it's not lying when we care for each other."

"Misleading them, then. Whatever you call it, it isn't honest."

"Mm. Now there's where you're wrong because what I feel for you is. Is that not true for you?"

Maybe that's what held her back. Could she do this, pretend and not fall for him in truth? Would her teenage crush and… and admiration bring stronger feelings? "Yes, but that doesn't mean I want you and Mac angry with each other because you both feel honor bound to protect me. He's angry, Ollie. Really angry."

"He just needs to let off some steam. No big brother likes the idea of his little sister kissing his best friend."

The flood of color made her feel hot and decidedly uncomfortable, but she couldn't deny the statement. "But it's fake," she repeated softly, refusing to admit the reminder was for herself.

"You're still his kid sister."

"Yeah, well, at the very least, he shouldn't think badly of you when I put this mess into motion. We should tell him. Mac wouldn't reveal the secret. I mean, hopefully we won't have to pretend for long but—"

"Let's wait and see then. Right now we have to take the next step."

"Which is?"

"We go out and be seen. Now that it's 'official,' it's time to be the couple about town."

"Do we have to?" When he gave her that look

of his, she rolled her eyes and groaned. "I know, I know."

"Is the thought of dating me that bad?"

"Of course not." Because honestly? She'd dreamed about it for years, which was no doubt why she'd blurted out his name and brought apocalyptic disaster upon them.

"Good. So how about we give those reporters something to write about?"

Chapter 6

Oliver held Marsali's quivering hand ten minutes later as they exited the house to a firestorm of shutter clicks and questions. He wanted to compliment her on the fact most women he knew would've taken at least an hour to prep for this event despite already being dressed and ready for the day but kept his comments to himself because he felt Marsali would slide into comparison mode again.

"Oliver! Oliver, any plans for filming more in Wilmington to spend time with Marsali?"

"Marsali, what's it like dating one of Hollywood's most eligible bachelors?"

"Oliver, are you angry that Marsali leaked the news of your dating?"

He squeezed her hand gently before fitting her

to his side and pausing outside of the passenger door of her vehicle. "Guys, give us some space, okay? We'll answer questions but back off a little." He glanced down at Marsali and lowered his head to kiss the top of hers. "Smile," he said for her ears only. "Give them what they want."

Marsali's arm tightened at his waist and she glanced up at him with those amazing eyes, giving him a shy smile that sent the cameras whirling.

"Oliver, exactly how long have you been dating?"

"When did things change between you?"

"What's it like dating the author of a dating guide for good girls after the women in Hollywood?"

The last question brought a round of chuckles from the reporters gathered around them, and Oliver knew not to touch that one with a ten-foot pole. "Okay, so, let me take a stab at some of those. Uh, no, I'm not upset with Marsali. She was under a lot of pressure, and Gwen had that photo cued up and ready to go, so it would've come out one way or another. Marsali and I have been close ever since her brother and I met freshman year in college, so it's just been a natural progression, I think," he said, smiling down at her and squeezing her side to urge her to nod, which she did.

"So you were dating when you last filmed in Wilmington? Was Marsali the reason for filming here?"

"Wilmington has a lot of potential for the film industry, but Marsali was definitely a bonus."

"Marsali, how are book sales? Since the news of your relationship was made public, have they gone up?"

"I don't know."

"You haven't checked?"

"No, I haven't."

"What about your clients? Are you getting busier now that the news is out you've snagged one of Hollywood's most elusive? Pretty good news for a matchmaker, right?"

"Um, calls have increased but—"

"Marsali is gifted when it comes to helping people find their special someone," Oliver said. "She always has been. If you know her history, she's been setting people up with successful matches since high school, and I'm glad she's finally getting recognition for her talents. Now, as much as we'd love to stand here, we're hungry. Guys, do me a favor and give us a break, okay? Dating is hard enough without all of you messing with my game."

A low chuckle ran through the reporters.

"Can we get personal interviews if we back off?" one of them asked.

Oliver opened the passenger door of Marsali's older-model Mercedes SUV but paused at the question. "Sure. Contact my agent to set things up. Just give us some time to get used to being public, okay?"

Marsali got into the vehicle, and he closed the door, lifting his hand to wave at the group and giving yet another photo op as he moved around the front to drive. It took him a moment to adjust the seat to fit his longer legs. "Keep smiling," he said to Marsali. "That wasn't so bad, was it?"

"They asked about my book sales and clients."

"Let them. Take advantage of the moment while it lasts."

"You're okay with that? They insinuated I'm using you to increase my business."

He started the engine. "So long as I know the truth, what does it matter?"

"It matters to me. It reflects badly on me and I don't like it."

Oliver shifted in the seat and stretched a hand

across the expanse, letting it settle on her nape under the thick warmth of her hair. He lightly gripped her and urged her toward him.

"What are you— *Now?*"

"Yes," he said, aware of the attention his behavior was getting from the reporters outside.

"I'm not sure I'm ready for this."

"The best thing to do," he said, closing the last bit of distance between them, "is dive in with both lips."

Shameless. That's what the voice in his head called him as Oliver used the situation to *his* advantage and kissed Marsali, not for the reporters or the attention it would bring, not even to help her, but because he wanted to. Now that he could touch her, kiss her, it was all he wanted to do.

He hoped that desire would never go away, and yet he knew he'd wish the opposite once their make-believe romance was over and he had to go back to just being her friend. For now, though, he'd take whatever contact he could get. Even though doing so probably meant another punch—or five —from Mac.

By the time he lifted his head, he'd forgotten all about the cameras in the windows snapping away.

Marsali ducked her head and let her wild curls

shield her face, and he put the car in reverse with a light honk of the horn.

He backed into the street and pulled away, noting that the majority of the reporters had gone to their vehicles parked along the street and appeared to be leaving. Between answering the questions and the kiss, they had something to run with for now. "Are you hungry?"

"No. All of this has me so nervous I've lost my appetite."

"Not even for the best burger in town?" He chuckled when she released a soft moan of appreciation for their favorite hangout.

"That actually does sound good, but how are we possibly going to eat in public? You'll be swarmed."

"You have to resign yourself and use it to your advantage. It'll disappear on its own fast enough once the novelty wears off." He'd much rather spend a quiet day alone with Marsali, but under the circumstances, that was as fictional as their dating status.

The drive to their favorite burger place took half the time it did during the tourist season. Their timing couldn't have been better, either, because they'd just missed the lunch rush. The guy behind the counter took their order without so much as a blink of recognition, but during the walk to their chosen table, Oliver heard a few whispers.

"People are staring," Marsali said.

"Does it bother you?"

"It's definitely not something I'm used to."

He held her chair for her and quickly settled himself into the seat opposite her. "Tell me about your new book deal. What's it about?"

She pursed her lips and shifted in her seat while removing her jacket.

"Do you need help?"

"No. I've got it, thanks. And the book deal—if I get it—is about maintaining the spark during a relationship. So many people see engagement or marriage as the end of romance. They've won the other person, so that's it. Done. My book idea talks about a woman's need for security and communication and all the forms that takes, as well as a man's needs in a relationship and how to keep the romance alive."

"So, love languages. That sort of thing?"

"You've read that book?"

"You recommended it, so, yeah. I did. And you make that sound far too easy to comprehend."

"It can be if the person is motivated to learn and wants his or her spouse to be happy."

"Motivation is good but I think the average guy would beg to differ on how easy that is."

"Oh? Why is that?"

He leaned toward her, taking in her sparkling eyes and beautiful face. He'd hoped the change in topic would get her mind off of the reporters and her family and all the chaos of her life right now, and it seemed to have worked. Marsali loved what she did, and she lit up a room when she talked about it. "Because the average guy doesn't think that way. Men aren't as complicated as women seem to want them to be."

"Men may not be complicated, but women are. And it's not just learning what women want but vice versa. If you have suggestions, I'd be happy to hear them."

"I hesitate to speak for all men, but I do believe women are more in tune with such things. It's easier for you."

"Maybe. But that's my point. Men can be just as tuned in if they're committed to getting to know someone on more than a physical level, and in doing so, it helps solidify a relationship and a deeper intimacy that keeps things interesting."

"Okay, Ms. Expert, how do I do that with you?"

Chapter 7

Marsali was saved from having to respond by their food order arriving. By the time the awestruck waitress delivered their meals and drinks, asked if they needed anything else, and lingered to the point of Oliver stating softly that he'd call her over if they needed her, the moment had passed. She hoped.

Because why give that kind of personal insight to a man who wasn't actually interested? "Oh, my word. I needed this," she said after taking a huge bite of her perfectly grilled mushroom burger.

Oliver dug in as well and they ate in silence for several minutes. Those seated inside the restaurant continued to shoot looks in their direction, but after a while, Marsali focused on her food and the man seated opposite her and nothing else. It was like a game, she realized. Though not one she was sure she wanted to play. Especially long term.

You only have yourself to blame.

She mentally groaned at the reminder. Maybe she should have used Mac's suggestion of stating her "relationship" with Oliver was in the past. Then the pretense wouldn't be necessary.

But it also wouldn't be nearly as fun.

It was her truth and she had to own it. The reason she'd said Oliver's name as her perfect match was because, to her, he was. Lock, stock, and barrel. Kind, considerate. Too gorgeous for words. But in that sense, he was the kind of gorgeous that made her nervous because of the attention it garnered from other women. Her mother was right—gah, she hated to admit it but it was true—Oliver's looks and career had a dark side.

But when it's a fake relationship, there's nothing to worry about.

And *that* was something she really had to keep repeating to herself and remember, otherwise when this was over and Ollie flew back to California, she was going to have a whole other problem on her hands—that of recovering from a broken heart. Because, truth be told, where Ollie was concerned, it could happen and she knew it.

"Hey. Where'd you go?"

The question forced her to focus and she managed a smile. "Sorry. I didn't sleep well and I think I zoned out."

"I'll try not to take that statement to heart as a reflection of my company."

She grinned at him and felt her heart squeeze a bit in return. "I don't think your ego needs stroking in that regard."

"Hmm. Debatable where you're concerned."

Wait, what?

"And don't think I didn't notice that you haven't answered my question yet. So tell me, how does one court a matchmaker? What does a man need to know about you?"

Staring into his dark eyes and that sexy scruff, she faltered. "Uh-uh. That's cheating."

"I have to find out on my own, eh?"

She shrugged and took a french fry she only let herself have when she ate here. Halfway to her lips, she second-guessed the choice given the fact the camera added ten pounds, and in the next few weeks, she'd undoubtedly be scrutinized for everything as Oliver's other half. "Um, any man worth his salt has to make the effort. We can't make it too easy on you—er, the man."

He cocked his head to one side and watched her.

"Eat that."

"Excuse me?"

"I can practically hear the debate from over here. Life is too short not to splurge here and there."

"That is not what my jeans say."

"Yeah, well, I'll argue that as a man, because the view I get is perfect."

Marsali felt her cheeks begin to heat, and she hated that she wore her embarrassment as boldly as she did her skinny jeans. "The camera adds weight, and so long as I'm hanging out with you, there are going to be *a lot* of cameras."

He snagged a fry from her plate and dipped it in ketchup before holding it up to her, and she was aware of the fact a few people in the restaurant held a phone pointed toward them. No doubt that was why Oliver did what he did, and in this moment, she needed to play along. "Fine."

She opened her mouth and let him feed her, forcing herself to focus on him and not the *awws* she heard from coming from another table that were soon followed by sighs and other comments.

"You know that'll be posted on social media before we can leave here."

"Then we'd better get going before word gets out we're here. Finish up."

She took a few more bites before declaring herself done and watched as Oliver left a generous tip on the table. They gathered up coats and headed toward the door, and Marsali realized she was alone because Oliver had paused by the cashier and handed her a card the girl scanned with adoring eyes.

"Here you go."

"Thanks. If anyone says anything, just tell them it was a thank you for letting us eat in peace."

He quickly ushered her out the door and to the car, and once inside, she stared at him. "You paid for everyone's food."

"Times are hard and there were several families in there with young kids. Hopefully it helps them. Seat belt."

She shook her head and grabbed the belt to latch it, wondering if Oliver would ever cease to appeal to her on levels he probably wasn't even aware of. But the whole nice-guy thing? Yeah, that was one of her boxes and he'd just checked it. "Now what?"

His phone pinged as though in response to her question, and Oliver pulled the device from his jacket pocket. He frowned at whatever it said before tucking it away.

"You up for a walk on the beach? The wind will be cold, but I haven't seen the surf since the last time I was here."

"Well, we need to fix that then. I'm always up for a walk on the beach." The wind off the water would leave her shivering, but sunshine and sand always lifted her mood and soothed frayed nerves.

Oliver got them moving once more and she found herself watching him drive. He took his time and wasn't one of those men gunning the engine every time he could or weaving in and out of traffic.

"Do you remember when I picked you up at that party in Wrightsville? You were… seventeen, I think?"

She groaned aloud and sank deeper into the passenger seat. "As much as I'd like to forget that night, yes, I remember. Mac was on a date, and I was panicking because I needed to get home for curfew and my friend had ditched me. I didn't know who else to call. Why?"

He was quiet a long time. So long she turned her head from the passing scenery to take in the profile Hollywood so loved. "What made you think of that night?"

"This, I guess. I'm glad you called me that night. And I'm glad you said my name in that interview."

His words brought a smile to her lips. "Yeah, well, I'm glad you've been so understanding considering the circumstances and craziness I've caused. Thank you, Ollie. I hope we'll always be friends. No matter what the future brings."

He stretched out his hand to grasp hers and carried it to his lips, pressing a kiss to her knuckles. "You don't have to do that when no one else is around."

His fingers tightened over hers before he released them.

"Right. Sorry."

Silence descended and she hated that she'd broken the ease of the moment. "Just staying in character, right?"

Of course he was. Oliver was an amazing actor. She'd been blown away the first time she'd seen him on-screen, and he'd only gotten better with every role since. No matter the part, the viewer felt the emotions portrayed.

And now here he was again, playing a role for her. But fact and fiction were wholly different, and it would be way too easy to allow herself to forget. To fall for the kisses and hand-holding and such when she would always be in the friend zone.

They had to keep up the illusion for those watching, but here, when they were alone, she needed to keep a proper distance to balance out the drugging kisses and those bedroom eyes of his.

She had to be realistic. People balked at her single status, thinking a single matchmaker didn't know her business. She could only imagine what they'd think if she were a brokenhearted—

"Oh, no."

"What? Something wrong?"

Panic filled her. Why hadn't she thought of that sooner? "What have we done?"

"Marsali?"

"It'll be *worse*."

"What will be worse?"

"This! We were so focused on the now we didn't talk about the future. Once we call things off, everyone will wonder why I couldn't keep you a-and make you happy. Why you left. Oh, why did we leave the house? I didn't think this through. Ollie, we've made a *huge* mistake."

Chapter 8

They went for a walk on the beach, and all the while, Oliver held her hand and reassured Marsali that everything was going to be okay. He managed to calm her panic attack by reminding her that they could only move forward, not back. And that Gwen had used the interview for sensationalism.

According to Oliver, nothing she'd said then or could say now would change public perception. As to what would happen when things ended, they'd come up with a plan to minimize the damage.

When they arrived back at her house, Marsali noted the reporters had returned, though they were fewer in number after receiving the guarantee of personal interviews. "Will they ever go away?"

"Free press is a plus. You said business is picking up, yeah?"

"Yes. Speaking of which, I've avoided my computer way too long. I should check in and see how things are going."

"Mind if I hang around? I can take care of Ginger for you while you work."

She smiled at him but shook her head in bemusement. "You wouldn't rather hang out with Mac?"

"I'm not dating Mac, sweetheart."

Ah. Yet another needed reminder that this was part of a role. "Of course. Come on in."

They exited the car and questions from the reporters bombarded them once again on the way inside. She'd just unlocked the front door when she heard one of them call out, louder than the others.

"Oliver, you've dated your share of women. What makes Marsali special?"

Marsali felt Oliver's hand tighten on her shoulder as he urged her inside.

"She just is. Now go home," he said. "We'll talk soon."

The moment the door shut behind them, Marsali breathed a sigh of relief. "I don't know how you deal with that everywhere you go."

"After a while, you don't see them anymore."

"Not possible," she said, removing her coat to hang it in the hall closet. She held out her hand for his, and Oliver took the hanger she held, their fingers brushing in the exchange.

A tingle raced through her, but she blamed it on her frazzled nerves and not anything remotely sexual.

Ginger heard their return and now barked and whined from inside her kennel, and Marsali used that as her excuse for hurrying by Oliver.

"I'll take Ginger out back to play. You go do what you need to do."

She paused, very aware of the fact this felt like a couple moment. Coming home, caring for Ginger. Even hanging their coats. It felt... intimate. "Thanks. But, um, watch her to make sure she potties. Oh, and she's still small enough to squeeze through the panels into Paul's yard if his gate is open. She's become quite the escape artist."

"I'll keep an eye on her."

Marsali forced her feet into motion and reminded herself that this—all of this—would be over very soon. She'd deal with whatever fallout came from it and mitigate what she could. It's all she could do.

She checked her computer and groaned at the number of messages from Claire. Her part-time assistant was quite capable, but apparently the majority of the callers insisted on speaking only to Marsali.

So were they future clients? Or reporters? How many were journalists pretending to be clients to get info she might unintentionally reveal? She hadn't considered that until this very moment, but it was probably something she would have to contend with in the next few weeks.

She heard Oliver exit the house with Ginger and glanced out the window to see the two of them playing in the yard. Oliver's easygoing grin as he hopped away from Ginger's playful paws as the dog chased after him left her sighing. The man really needed to come with a warning label. *Caution: will cause unrealistic fantasies.*

Because what woman wouldn't want to see him in her home every day? Across from the dinner table? In her bed?

Her cell pinged and she flipped it over to stare at the screen.

I don't agree with what you're doing but I'm here if you need me.

She tapped on the screen to open the texting window and replied to Mac. *I love you, too.*

You and Oliver are all over social media. Nice lunch?

She winced at the news but knew it was bound to happen. *Great lunch. The fries were delicious.*

Maybe that last line wasn't necessary, but if Mac was going to dish it out, she had to give a little back. It wouldn't be normal if she didn't.

Just be careful. It might seem fun now, but there could be consequences you haven't considered.

An uneasy knot twisted in her stomach. *Like?*

Just be careful.

The door to the living room opened, and Oliver entered and called Ginger inside. The dog quickly tumbled over Oliver's feet and then sat, staring up at him with adoring eyes and a big puppy grin. Oh, not good.

Even her dog was falling for Ollie.

Still, she doubted Ginger was what Mac referenced when he'd issued the warning.

OLIVER DISCOVERED he liked the quiet peace of spending the evening with Marsali. The last time he was in town was for his friends' parents' anniversary dinner, and while he'd seen and spent time with

Marsali, it was mostly from a distance due to all the party preparations.

She'd looked amazing that night in an off-the-shoulder sundress. He'd never realized how sexy collarbones could be until he'd found himself wanting to know more about hers.

He'd managed to snag a few dances with her during the course of the night, but she had proven as popular as he had when it came to the other singles in the room.

A little while later, Oliver rolled to his feet after gently nudging Ginger aside and stood, earning Marsali's attention. "You're working hard over there."

"Sorry. I can't believe how many emails have come in. I'm trying to help my assistant schedule everything. I'm just not sure when there will be time, because no one wants to wait. I'll have to put Ginger into doggy day care because I'll be gone so much."

He smiled to himself, pleased that, if nothing else, his presence had helped her business. Not that she needed much help. Marsali had proven herself over the years as a smart, capable woman. But just as quickly, a thought formed and he frowned. "Does your assistant go with you for the interviews?"

"No, why?"

He opened his mouth to comment but quickly decided to apologize later rather than argue about the phone call he planned to make to Guardian Group. While he'd like to think all of the people were legitimate and genuinely looking for dating help, he had to consider the alternative and be proactive. "Just wondering. I'm getting hungry again. Would you mind if I check out the fridge? I could grill us something or order delivery if you'd rather."

Her eyes widened when she glanced at the clock on the wall.

"Oh, wow. I had no idea it was getting so late. I've really been a bad host."

"Not at all. Ginger and I have had fun. On that last trip, we, un, visited with Paul for a bit."

"She got away from you, didn't she?"

He grinned at her and shrugged. "I think Paul liked having the company."

"I'm sure he did. I can't forget that lasagna," she said, grabbing a notepad to make a note of it.

He watched her and thought of how good the world would be if everyone was as kind and considerate as Marsali. "You know, I rarely get evenings where I just get to hang out and relax. Thank you for that."

Marsali tilted her head to one side as she regarded him, and he found himself moving closer, simply because he couldn't help himself.

"Is it so hard being a super-hot Hollywood movie star?"

He laughed softly due to the twinkling he saw in her eyes. That teasing, that grin made him want to kiss her and not stop anytime soon. "Depends on your definition of hard. I've sacrificed certain freedoms, for sure. Like ninety percent of my privacy." And a bit of safety, which was why he'd be calling to see if Denz was available. If not Denz, then someone else.

"Wow. Way to sell it," she said wryly.

"I make it work," he said simply, clapping his hands together and rubbing. "Now, food. I'm in the mood to whip up something that'll make your toes curl. Any special requests before I head back to my hotel?"

Chapter 9

The following evening, Oliver let himself into the unlocked back door of the closed gym. He had dropped Marsali off at her house after dinner at a local cafe and realized during their time there that he needed to step up his game in his role as her boyfriend after spotting the restaurant's decorations.

Valentine's Day rapidly approached, and given the circumstances and press they were receiving, he knew people were paying attention. No way could the day go by without some highly visible romancing. Marsali's matchmaker career made it doubly important. Not that he minded.

Once Marsali had completed the things she needed to do that day, he'd insisted on taking her and Ginger for a walk on the beach before the sun set.

He didn't think either of them were recognizable with their sunglasses and toboggan hats on to combat the cold breeze off of the water, but he wanted Marsali to know that life could be fairly normal. In LA he went grocery shopping and ran his own errands. With so many celebrities in one location, it was the norm.

The walk was nice. Oliver focused on the simple pleasures of watching Ginger play in the sand and holding Marsali's hand. The feel of her small palm in his had been a blessing and a curse, and in the silence of the drive to the gym, he realized it was because somewhere along the way he'd stopped pretending.

Or, more likely, he'd never started.

Touching her, kissing her had brought every thought he'd ever had about her to the surface. He found himself struggling to remember this was a temporary situation and not something he could allow himself to get used to, whereas Marsali didn't seem to have that problem. She'd made several comments about his impending return to Hollywood as well as the roles she believed they both played.

But now he knew his time of reckoning had come, a fact confirmed once he'd opened the door and heard the painful-sounding punches connecting with a heavyweight bag. He turned the corner into the main area and spotted his best friend midway across the room. "That bag supposed to be me?"

Mac paused and turned to face Oliver briefly before steadying the bag again.

"What do you think?"

Oliver continued closer despite the wariness he felt. He didn't want to be at odds with Mac, especially now. "Is the idea of us dating that hard to wrap your head around? I care for Marsali. I always have."

"That's the one thing I don't doubt." *Punch.* "What I doubt are your reasons."

"Come on, Mac. Marsali and I have always been friends. We've always been close."

"Not that close," Mac drawled. "I don't know when things changed but obviously they have. Friendship I'm fine with, but more?" Mac paused again and held up a gloved hand in Oliver's direction. "No freaking way."

"Mac—"

"This isn't a game, Oliver. And she certainly isn't some Hollywood hookup. Now get in the ring."

"So you can beat on me? I have a premier coming up." It was an obnoxious reason for not doing as Mac ordered but the only one Oliver could think of to keep from having to hit his best friend—or becoming Mac's punching bag.

"Don't be a wuss. If you insist, I won't hurt your pretty face. I'll just pound on the rest of you."

"Look, call me anything you want. I know you're angry. But if we beat on each other, Marsali will have both our heads on a platter. Do you really want to have to listen to that lecture?"

Marsali had given them both a few speeches over the years. Mostly about girls and where the guys fell short when it came to whatever problem they were having at the time. It was rare for him and Mac to have an argument, but whenever they did, Marsali had always been the peacemaker, lecturing them until they gave in just to get her to hush.

"I'll take my punishment. Now put the gear on or do without, but one way or another, I'm going to remind you of why it's not wise to date within certain circles."

"Marsali doesn't need us fighting each other right now."

"She doesn't *need* you groping her, either."

"Mac—"

"You swore to me you'd leave my sister alone!"

He had. He'd promised sixteen years ago when Mac had insisted on it. "She was a kid in high school then."

"Doesn't matter."

"It does. She's a grown woman now. Besides, you know I'd never intentionally hurt her."

"What I know is that you're taking advantage of someone who isn't on your level, man. She's… The girl didn't even know what *Netflix and chill* meant until I told her."

Oliver tried hard not to laugh but the sound came out despite his best efforts. "She's sweet, Mac. Innocent. I *like* that about her."

"She's a romantic with her head in the clouds, and you need to leave her alone."

"Why? Am I not good enough for her? I'm not, I'll readily admit that, brother, but I'm not some loser off the street. I can give her—"

"Nothing but pain," Mac interjected.

Oliver swallowed hard, his hands fisting at his sides. "Is it because of my past? Where I come from?"

Mac bit out a curse that would've had the women in his family scolding him.

"Seriously?"

"What else am I supposed to think?"

"Oliver, you had a rough start but that's not what this is about. Had you and Marse gotten together *before* Hollywood came calling, that'd be one thing, but now? You chose your path and it comes with a lot of trouble and problems she doesn't need to be a part of. Now I'm asking you to leave Marsali alone."

"I can't."

Mac let loose a curse and pummeled the bag with short, quick jabs that rocked it, not stopping until he was out of breath. That done, Mac whirled away from the bag and charged Oliver. He couldn't get a grip on him because of the boxing gloves, but he used brute force to throw Oliver back against the nearby ring.

"Marsali isn't the only thing on the line. If you hurt her, we're done. You hear me? How many of those Hollywood buddies of yours will ever have your back the way I have all these years?"

"None of them," Oliver said, holding Mac's gaze as he made the statement.

Mac lifted his hands and bounced them off of Oliver's chest.

"Exactly. You're walking a tightrope, *Ollie*. You fall off and nobody's gonna be there to catch you."

Oliver took the warning to heart. The last thing he wanted was to lose Mac when true friends were so hard to come by. Especially one who'd been a brother to him from day one.

Mac shoved away from Oliver with a frustrated growl and paced across the floor, punching the air like he couldn't help himself.

"Get geared up and in the ring."

Mac kicked a set of gloves at him.

Oliver bent to retrieve the gear and held the gloves to his chest, jogging backwards to start warming up, because at this point, he knew he had to take a few knocks to let Mac get it out of his system. "You gotta calm down, man. Stress will kill you."

Mac said something unseemly and Oliver grinned and pulled on the first glove. "Look, just try to accept it, okay?"

"And why should I do that?"

Oliver used his teeth to tighten the second glove and did a few test jabs to get them fitted comfortably. "Are you really going to make me fight you over this? Can't we just call it and find a game to watch somewhere?"

Mac's smile served as a warning, and Oliver swallowed hard, glad he'd spent the last twelve months training with one of the best martial arts experts in the world while filming his latest and had continued to practice since.

"You tell Marsali about meeting me?"

"No."

"Even better. We'll see how good of an actor you are when it comes to hiding the pain you're gonna feel for breaking the code and putting the moves on my baby sister."

They got in the ring, and after a few more minutes warming up, the two of them began sparring. Oliver let Mac get a few shots in, figuring they were well deserved for his true thoughts about Marsali, but after the third one connected, Oliver put the twelve months of martial arts training to use and took Mac down, using a wrestling hold to keep him there.

Mac's curses filled the gym, and once he was out of steam, Oliver leaned low. "You're going to feel really bad about this."

"What makes you think that?" Mac griped into the padded floor as he struggled to free Oliver's hold.

"Because." He told himself to keep his mouth

shut and not do the very thing he'd warned Marsali against, but he sighed and said, "It's fake."

Mac stopped struggling.

"What?"

Oliver released Mac and jumped back before Mac's legs could connect and take him down.

"What's fake?" Mac demanded.

"Look, it's a secret and one you're sworn to keep, okay? I mean it. Marsali's career is on the line here, so unless you're willing to pay her bills and give her a new life, you won't discuss what I'm about to say with anyone."

"Just say it already."

Oliver explained how Marsali had come to say his name on air.

"Wait, so you flew here to—"

"To talk to Marsali in person to find out what had happened, and we came up with a plan."

"To fake date."

"Until she can get some things settled with her clients and the new book deal, yeah."

"Then what? How does this end well for her?"

The comment reminded Oliver of Marsali's panic attack as they'd headed toward the beach, and even though he had his own ideas on the best ending, he had to stick with the program. "Look, just give it a few weeks. As soon as some socialite gets spotted with someone triple her age, the attention will shift off of Marsali and we can quietly dissolve. At most… maybe a couple of months," he said.

"*Months*?"

"Hey, I'm a movie star. It's gonna have to be pretty scandalous to top me."

Mac's expression left Oliver chuckling for a moment, but when his friend continued to stare, Oliver became uneasy. "What?"

"Why are you really doing this?"

"I just told you."

Mac shook his head.

"No. Uh-uh. I'm not buying it. That may have been how this whole mess came about, but you have *always* had a thing for her. Don't stand there and tell me you haven't."

Oliver ripped off a glove and tossed it to the floor. "I'm just helping her, man."

"Yeah, but why? See, that's the thing. Because I think you're doing all of this hoping it'll turn into more for real. Am I right?"

Chapter 10

The following Monday morning, Marsali knocked softly on Oliver's hotel room door in Carolina Cove and waited for him to answer. She told herself it was because she wanted to check on him and not because she'd woken up this morning feeling as though she physically *needed* his presence.

But having spent the majority of the last two days with him, that was exactly what it had felt like. *Not good, Marsali. Not good.*

She heard a sound on the other side of the door and a slight scrape that might indicate the portal over the peephole being slid back. She stared at the metal ring, aware of the exact moment the lock clicked out of place.

Marsali braced herself as the door swung wide.

"Hey. I wasn't expecting you."

Marsali opened her mouth to respond, and her greeting came out mortifyingly husky as she said a choked hello.

She'd seen Oliver shirtless plenty of times over the years. From his less brawny, early college days hanging out in her parents' pool to his sweaty, oiled, and very masculine scenes on-screen. But seeing him all big and broad and strong in person now? It took effort to unglue her tongue from the roof of her mouth. "Um, did I interrupt your workout?"

The soft gym shorts hung low on his hips, and he wore a light sheen of sweat. She found herself having to forcibly turn her head to study the furnishings of the hotel so that she didn't ogle him like one of the fangirls Mac had so recently accused her of being.

"I'm finished so it's all good. That for us?"

"What? Oh, yes," she said, remembering the items in her clenched hands. "If you want it. I wasn't sure if it's on your meal plan. I know you… watch that," she said, realizing her gaze had drifted to his six-pack once more.

She forced her gaze high and found him smiling as he watched her. Of course Oliver would find her funny. He was no doubt used to women much more sophisticated and able to keep themselves focused no matter his state of dress—or undress.

"I appreciate it. Thanks. I was going to wait and grab something on my way to see you, but whatever that is will be perfect."

"Do you, um, think maybe you could put on a shirt?"

His low, husky chuckle warmed her insides and brought a hot flush of color rushing into her face she couldn't hide if she tried.

Oliver moved toward her with that lazy, movie-star stride of his and didn't stop until he stood far too close for comfort. She wanted to take a step back but refused to let herself retreat. She was a strong, confident woman, after all. Just not a—

"Why, Marsali… am I a distraction to you?"

"Um…"

"It's good to know the feeling is mutual," he said, lowering his head and kissing her cheek. "Good morning, beautiful."

Wait. What? "Oliver, I told you, you don't have to do that when no one is around, remember?"

"Ollie."

She blinked at him and frowned. "What?"

"You call me Ollie, not Oliver."

"Ollie," she said, his name emerging as a whisper. She cleared her throat and struggled to focus. "Um, there are reporters out front. And a bunch of fans. Hotel security is keeping them out as best they can but…"

"Marsali? Breathe. I'm going to compliment you whenever I want," he said. "And, yeah, the concierge called me to fill me in. Did you have any problem with the hotel staff letting you up?"

"No. No problem. I, um, had a client interview this morning at London's Lattes. After the meeting, though…"

"What?"

She inhaled but she couldn't shrug off the awareness she'd felt. "I'm sure it's nothing. I'm probably just being paranoid, and it's probably one of the reporters but—"

"Marsali, just say it."

"I think someone followed me. He got to the coffee shop right after I did, sat there while I conducted the interview, but when I left, he followed me here to the inn, and when I got on the elevator, he was walking toward them, too. It was… weird."

A knock sounded on the door and she startled.

"It's okay," Oliver said. "Hang tight."

Oliver walked over and looked out the peephole before opening the door.

"Good timing. Come on in."

"Is she here?" the man from the coffee shop asked. He wore tan slacks and a pullover and carried a leather jacket.

"Yeah."

Marsali stared up at the handsome man, noting that he stood taller and broader than Oliver. "Oliver, what's going on?"

"Marsali, I'd like you to meet Denz. Denz, Marsali Jones."

"Nice to meet you, Ms. Jones," the man said in his deep voice.

"I… Marsali. It's nice to meet you." She looked to Oliver for answers and found he seemed hesitant. "Were you just… How do you know each other?"

Denz looked at Oliver, both eyebrows raised as he waited for Oliver to answer.

"Denz is a bodyguard."

"Oh. I didn't realize. I thought you only needed one for big events," she said, remembering a conversation between her, Mac, and Oliver in the past when they'd discussed photos of him with various guards whenever he filmed overseas or in a large city setting.

According to Oliver, actors were a dime a dozen in Hollywood, and the only time bodyguards were needed there was if the star was controversial. So in his case, he occasionally needed one during fan-based events but that was it.

"He's not for me, Marsali. I asked Denz to come to Wilmington to keep an eye on you."

She blinked at the clarification. "Um. *Why?*" she said, ignoring the fact her voice quivered with her upset. She didn't need someone following her around like some—

"For safety. Why else?"

"I've been threatened?"

"No. But it occurred to me that with all of the new clients you're taking on, some might not have the best of intentions. Better safe than sorry. Denz is with Guardian Group, a protection and investigative service I'm familiar with. You can trust him."

She paced to the far side of the room, aware of both men watching her and very uncomfortable with that fact. "This is crazy. I do not need a bodyguard. If he should be guarding someone, it's you. You're the Hollywood star."

"Marsali, you won't even know he's there," Oliver said.

"I knew. I told you he—"

"Because he let you," Oliver said. "Which makes me wonder why?" he asked, looking at Denz.

"She picked up a gawker leaving the coffee shop, so I wanted it known she wasn't alone."

Marsali felt the weight of their stares once again and faltered. A "gawker"? She hadn't noticed anyone. "Really?"

"Yeah. Beady-eyed little guy about your height. Thick glasses. When he realized you weren't alone, he took off."

And isn't that the point?

The thought of being followed freaked her out, but the thought of being *unaware* she was being followed creeped her out even more. "I didn't see him. Um, thank you, I guess."

"Why don't I step out and give you two some time," Denz said. "I'll be in the hall if you need me."

"Thanks, Denz," Oliver said.

Oliver walked Denz to the door and then leaned against it momentarily once it was closed, his gaze wary when it met hers.

"I should've told you I was calling him. I planned to tell you about Denz when I saw you today," he said. "But I'm not sorry. Not when he's already proven necessary."

Necessary. Because of her involvement with Oliver. Oh, she so wasn't sure she could do this.

"Marsali?"

She moved to the window and stared out at the Atlantic below. The beach was mostly empty, but there were several bundled up against the February wind to get their sand and surf fix. "I get it, Ollie. I don't like it," she said bluntly, "but I get it. I'll be more careful. It's so pretty outside that I left my car at the shop and walked here, but next time I'll drive."

"Good idea. And remember, it won't be forever. Once things die down, Denz won't be necessary."

She nodded and struggled to take a fortifying breath. "So, um, Claire said the press interviews are being confirmed with your agent, so she's rearranging some client interviews on my end. Claire also said your agent didn't exactly sound thrilled at the thought of us doing interviews together since they're for the premiere and not our romance, my book, or my business."

Oliver moved to stand behind her. She felt his presence before his hands settled on her shoulders and slid down her arms in a soothing gesture.

"Do you care what she thinks?"

"She's important to you. To *your* career. So, yes."

"Rikki will get over it. According to her, actors are more attractive if they're single but that doesn't mean she's right. Nor do I care. She has nothing to do with why I'm here or why I'm staying."

Marsali released the lower lip she worried between her teeth. "I'm causing you problems, Ollie."

"Nothing I can't handle."

"Are you sure? Because I also texted Mama last night after you left my house, and she said Mac was meeting you at the gym."

"We came to terms, that's all."

She turned to face him and took in his bare chest and broad shoulders, but other than rock-hard abs and a light smattering of chest hair, she saw no damage. "Do I want to know what those terms are?"

"That I don't hurt you. You know I wouldn't, right? Not deliberately."

She stared up into those dark eyes of his and wondered if it was possible not to be hurt by him. "I know."

"You should also know that I told Mac the truth."

Shocked rolled through her. "You did? But you said—"

"That we'd wait and see. I know. But I told him. Mac knows how important it is that we keep this secret, though."

"Lies, bodyguards, secrets," she murmured. "This is getting very complicated, Ollie. I hate the deception."

"Me, too. I had a thought about that last night after I got back here, too."

She was so afraid to ask. "Oh?"

"Yeah. I got to thinking about you, and me, and since it's bothering us both, why not end the lie by making it real?"

"Excuse me?" She couldn't have heard him correctly. Did he just say—

"Marsali, what if we didn't pretend? What if we played this out? See where it could lead? What could happen? Would that be such a bad thing?"

"I… Seriously?"

"Is it that crazy of an idea?"

She blinked at him, unsure of what to say when she seriously wondered if she hadn't actually woken up yet this morning and this was all a dream. A really sweet, unbelievably sexy, totally weird dream. "Um…"

"Unless you don't… like me that way. Is that it?"

Heaven help her. Had he just asked that question of *her*? Not like him? Seriously? "I-I do. I mean, Ollie, this is… It's a surprise. I'm a little confused. No, not really. I'm a lot confused," she said.

"About what?"

A huff left her and she struggled to form words. "Well, if you've felt that way, why haven't you said anything before now? Are you sure this doesn't have anything to do with—" A thought formed and she took a step back from the overwhelming sight that Oliver was. "Mac? Is this some weird *guy* thing? Mac said something and you're feeling guilty now and that's why you're… Ollie, no. No, we are *not* doing this."

She turned away from him and headed toward the door, but halfway there, he gently caught her arm and held, stopping her in her tracks.

"This is between you and me, Marsali," he said, tugging her stiff body gently toward him.

Her hands flattened against his chest and heat seared her, shooting through her body like a rocket. How could his chest be so hard and soft at the same time? How could he smell so good when he was post-workout and hadn't showered yet?

When am I going to wake up?

"This has nothing to do with Mac. Okay? This is me, wondering if the girl I've wanted to kiss since the moment I first laid eyes on her has ever felt the same way."

The moment he first…? "That's impossible."

He stared down at her with his piercing gaze, and her heart pounded hard in her chest. The way he looked at her… The expression on his face as he waited for her to…

"Why is that so impossible?"

"Because I was a high school freshman a-and a hot mess."

"You were… a freshman," he clarified, a gentle smile forming on his gorgeous face. "But definitely not a hot mess. What you were was too young and I had a lot left to figure out."

"Fine. But what about since then? Ollie, it's been years. You've had plenty of—"

"By the time you turned sixteen, Mac had caught on to my interest and me wanting to join him whenever he came home from college. He made it clear friends didn't cross the line when it came to little sisters. I had to promise to keep my hands to myself."

She winced at the news and wondered if Mac had ever known just how hard she'd fallen for his friend over the years. "But if that's the case, why are you speaking up now? You and Mac are still friends... Aren't you?"

Oliver slid his hand under her chin and lifted her face higher, and she caught her breath when his thumb brushed over her lower lip.

"We are. But he also thinks we're pretending."

"So we'd be lying about our lie." She tucked her chin to her chest and groaned.

"Marsali, I know this is hard but... I'm thinking life is too short to let this slip away. When I heard you say my name during that interview... I don't know, I guess I thought maybe this was our chance. So, what do you say to making us the real deal?"

She opened her mouth but no words formed, because she thought about the book she'd written on dating for good girls and the details and bound- aries laid out within. Lines she believed shouldn't be crossed until vows were exchanged. How did Holly- wood fit in that scenario?

It doesn't. "You... I don't... Oliver, I don't know."

His gaze narrowed on her and she got the impression she'd hurt him. But if that was true, that meant he did mean what he said and... "This is a lot. There is so much to consider. I-I mean your career and mine and how this would work, a- and... I'm not one of those women. I'm not... the women you're used to who'll do whatever, whenever. *Hollywood* women who... I'll *never* be one of them."

"If I wanted one of them, I'd be with them. Marsali—"

"I won't fit in. You'll grow tired of me and want someone more like one of them, and I'll try to make you happy but I'll resent you wanting me to change and—"

"Sweetheart?"

"Oh, Ollie, it would never wor—"

He lowered his head and kissed her but this time the kiss was different. He was different. She felt his hand fist in her hair and gasped against his mouth, giving him the invitation he needed and took full advantage of.

In the space of seconds, she went from standing strong and firm on her own confused feet to sagging against him and clinging to him like a vine. A breathless, trembling, can-this-be-happening mess who struggled to remember her own name by the time he lifted his head. It took her still longer to realize the "practice" kisses they'd shared were a seriously watered-down version of those he'd held in check, because this... *this* was the difference between Oliver the actor and *Ollie*.

"Marsali, I don't want anyone else," he said. "I

want you. Even if it means Mac gets angry for a while and we have to kiss up to him to get his forgiveness. I'll do it. I'll do whatever it takes. Let's see where this can go."

Marsali stared up at him. The lump in her throat made it hard to breathe, because she knew saying yes would bring nothing but trouble and saying no would mean she'd always, *always* wonder.

She cleared her throat and fought off the surge of panic sliding through her and decided that, if nothing else, dating Oliver in truth was a once-in-a-lifetime opportunity she just couldn't pass up. "Um, okay."

"Yeah?"

"Yeah, let's— Oh!"

He lifted her up off her feet and swirled her around and she held on to his broad shoulders and laughed. By the time her feet touched the floor, he'd lowered his head to kiss her, and the world and all of its problems disappeared with the touch of his lips on hers. "Mmm," she said against his mouth. "Wait. W-we can't tell Mac," she said when she regained a little bit of sanity. "If we do this, he can't know."

"Marsali—"

"I won't have him hating you and angrier than

he already is and... we don't know the future, so why upset Mac even more if things don't work out? He thinks we're pretending so just... let him. Please?"

She could tell Oliver didn't like her statement or the hesitation loaded within it, but after a long moment, he nodded. "Okay." He smoothed his hand over her hair. "We won't tell him."

"Thank you."

Oliver was silent a moment, then inhaled.

"Do you have plans today?"

"Yeah. More new client interviews later this afternoon. I had Claire squeeze as many of them in as she could before we have to do the ones you promised the press."

"Denz will go, too. He'll stay out of your way so long as he doesn't feel there's danger. Okay?"

Her thoughts must have shown on her face, because his mouth took a downward turn.

"Look, I know it's weird having a stranger tailing you but it's just to be safe. You can't argue with that, right?"

"I suppose. Oliver..."

He drew her close and kissed her again. "What?"

"I can't stay here in your hotel room for long.

People will talk. Can we eat this downstairs?" People would talk regardless of where they ate, but she knew for her own sake and business brand that she needed to stand firm on some things.

Oliver stared at her a few seconds as though unable to believe it would be an issue, but after a moment, he nodded.

"Give me five more minutes to shower," he said against her lips before releasing her.

Oliver headed for the bathroom and Marsali stood awkwardly in his hotel suite. The view drew her once more and she moved to the window.

The last thing she wanted was to do something that would end her friendship with Oliver. She'd rather have his friendship for the rest of her life and deny herself than…

Risk losing him forever.

Was this wise?

Too late now.

She inhaled a shuddering breath and left the window only to pause by the desk. The front page of the newspaper had a picture of her and Oliver walking hand in hand on the beach. Another, smaller picture taken from their burger-and-fry lunch date appeared below it.

Outside in the hallway, she heard Denz's deep

voice as he spoke to someone. Yet another intrusion into her life.

Dating Oliver came at a cost higher than that of her family's opinion and upset. It meant no privacy. No true boundaries, because as far as other people were concerned, their private life was fair game.

When added *to* her family drama when Mac learned the truth…

Was she really ready for this?

Chapter 11

Oliver made a quick phone call to his assistant in California before jumping in the shower. Marsali's acceptance of their change in status meant more to him than she'd ever know, and a celebration was in order, however brief it had to be due to her next appointment.

Making arrangements didn't take long, thanks to an assistant who knew how to work worldwide via a few clicks of the keyboard and phone calls. It also didn't hurt that he was able to use Oliver's name. Sometimes fame had its advantages.

Denz slid behind the wheel of a rental while Oliver ushered Marsali into the large SUV. They headed toward the marina address sent by Sam, his assistant.

"What are we doing here?"

"You'll see. You said you have a couple of hours free so… let's go."

Denz parked and Oliver took Marsali's hand to lead the way to the charter his assistant had booked for them.

"Really?"

He grinned at her excitement and squeezed her hand gently. "What is it with you and boats?"

"They're just so cool," she said, a laugh bubbling out of her. "I never understood how my dad could live here and not own one."

"He probably knew you and Mac would be joyriding on it if he did," he said, turning to steady her once he'd made it aboard. "Safer to have a friend with a boat than to own one himself. If you get too cold, I'll be happy to keep you warm," he added, not letting go of her until he saw the flush rise in her cheeks once more.

That was the thing he loved about Marsali. When he looked at her, touched her, kissed her, she responded in such a sweet, insanely hot way that turned him on like nothing and no one else ever had.

"Welcome. Mr. Beck, it's nice to meet you. I hope you don't mind my saying so, but I'm a fan.

I've seen all your movies. Miss," the captain said, dipping his head in greeting.

"Thanks, I'm glad you've enjoyed them. This is my girlfriend, Marsali Jones."

"A pleasure to meet you, miss. It's a beautiful day to be on the water, but if you get chilled, there are blankets and windbreakers laid out below."

"That's great. Thank you, Captain," she said.

"Everything has arrived, Mr. Beck, and is ready and waiting for you."

"Great. Ms. Jones has an appointment in Carolina Cove at three, so we'll need to be back in plenty of time for that," he said.

"No problem, sir. I'll get us underway. Enjoy, and if you need anything, you let me or Justin know," the captain said.

Justin looked all of twenty and a little star-struck as he showed them below deck. Lunch had been set up in front of the floor-to-ceiling windows of the luxury yacht, giving them a break from the wind and cooler temp while they ate.

"Oh, Ollie," Marsali breathed softly as she stared at the interior.

He realized then that he'd grown a little too accustomed to things like this, whether it be via his friends' yachts or trailers on a set that cost more than ninety-five percent of the homes in America. It wasn't a pleasant thought, and he vowed then and there to do a better job at remembering his roots. "Do you like it?"

She gave him a look that made it clear his assistant had done well in answering his request.

"It's beautiful. All of it."

"Come on, let's eat. I'm hungry."

"You're always hungry."

"Hey, I burn a lot of calories in those workouts. And this is a treat I think you'll like even more than the boat if I remember correctly."

"Are you ready to be served?" Justin asked.

Oliver seated Marsali at the well-appointed table just as the engine started with a low growl of power. Justin emerged from somewhere with a rolling cart of dome-covered plates and a bottle of champagne.

"I know it's early, but we're celebrating," Oliver said.

"Would you like to do the honors?" Justin asked Oliver.

"Yeah, I got it. Thanks, Justin." Oliver set to work on the bottle of Dom Perignon and smiled at Marsali's laugh when the cork popped. He poured them both a glass and lifted his toward her. "To us."

Marsali clinked her glass to his, and they gazed into each other's eyes as they sipped.

"So what's under here?" she asked, eyeing the silver cover closest to her.

"I'm beginning to think your love language is gifts or surprises," he said, referring to one of their previous conversations.

"Hmm. I do like them," she said.

His gaze shifted to the curl on her full lips and he immediately wondered what she'd taste like now after the champagne. "I'll add that to the list along with puppies and boat rides. What else do you like?"

"Ah, you're trying to cheat again. You have to figure it out by sheer observation."

"Okay, if that's the case. Gifts and quality time. Now, tell me what I like." He'd asked the question half-heartedly, not really expecting more than a general response, but Marsali's cheeks began to flush and he realized... Oh, man.

"You like... puppies."

"Now who's cheating? Most everyone likes puppies. Come on, what are mine?"

"Words of affirmation and physical touch," she stated confidently.

"Mmm. Anything else?"

"You, um, also like your steak cooked medium

rare, you hate pickles but love olives, and… you… seem to like me."

He leaned forward in his chair. "Oh, that is definitely true."

"See? I'm good. Can we eat? This smells heavenly."

"Have at it," he said, watching while she removed the cover. Her lips parted with a gasp when she spied the shrimp scampi beneath. He grabbed the top of the larger dome in the middle of the table and revealed a pile of crab legs.

"Oh, my word."

"Still your favorite?"

"Oh, yeah. Lord, bless it, and let's eat."

He laughed at her excitement and handed the covers off to Justin. "That's my girl."

Half an hour later, he watched as she finished her dessert, and it took everything in him not to order the captain to marry them. Was that still a thing? Being able to marry at sea? Did the Intercoastal Waterway count?

All he knew was that he'd enjoyed himself more in the last couple of days spent with Marsali than he had in years. Maybe his lifetime.

He shifted out of his chair and snagged her hand, lifting it to his lips to get a taste. Her gorgeous eyes darkened as he swirled his tongue and gently sucked the buttery goodness from her fingertip. He kept hold of her hand and braced his free hand on the chair at her back, leaning low to capture her lips with his.

She tasted like salt and butter and the miniature New York style cheesecake she'd just consumed. The kiss deepened because he couldn't help himself, and he tugged her up out of her chair, letting his fingers slide up her back to tangle in her long curls.

Marsali ended the kiss with a gasp, and he pressed a kiss to her forehead and lingered over the contact. "You," he whispered huskily, "like romance."

A low huff left her that sounded more than a little sarcastic.

"Totally obvious observation—like knowing each other's food choices after being friends for so long."

"Mmm. But this is different. You like old-fashioned romance. The kind that's real and honest and wholesome. Holding hands and kissing, flirting. You like it when I tug on your hair and kiss your neck," he said, doing just that.

"You," she whispered, "I-like making me blush."

He lifted his head and skimmed a finger lightly

over her soft cheek. "You're right about that, sweet-heart. I would love to know what naughty thoughts run through that sweet head of yours."

She stared up at him a long moment, lips parted. More often than not, he had some sense of what she was thinking, but right now, here, she kept him wondering.

"We should, um, go up top before it's too late and we have to head back."

Was that her way of cooling him down? Was she afraid he'd press her for more even though, having read her book, he knew her limits when it came to dating and sex?

Chapter 12

The following few weeks were filled with television, radio, and podcast interviews for them because of Oliver's upcoming premiere and their newsworthy romance.

Oliver sensed Marsali's tension and hesitation and knew she worried about saying something she shouldn't. He found himself staring at her like a lovesick teenager, much to his hosts' enjoyment, but he watched with pride as Marsali became more confident with every exchange.

Now Oliver entered through the back door of her house with Ginger at his heels and moved through the room to her kitchen. "Chow time, eh, girl?"

He found the dog's food and measured out the

allotted amount, then made sure she had fresh water. The dog got so excited over her dinner her back end danced with every wag of her tail.

"I'm going to miss seeing her do that," Marsali said from behind him.

"Does that mean you're not going to keep her?"

"I don't know."

He turned to find Marsali leaning against the doorframe to her kitchen and frowned. "Hey, you okay?"

"Hmm? Oh, yeah. I'm fine."

She didn't sound very convincing. "Marsali, if something is going on, you can tell me."

She shook her head.

"I just got off the phone with Mama."

Again? He braced himself for whatever came next. "I should've gone to see them."

"In Florida? We don't need their permission, Ollie."

"No, but it's not like I'm a stranger out of nowhere."

"Exactly. They already know you, so it's no big deal."

"Except that it is?" He moved closer to her and drew her into his arms, snuggling her against him, very aware of the tension-filled sigh she released when he rubbed her back and shoulders. "You can't blame them for worrying. They love you."

"I know but worrying and smothering are a fine line."

"Their love for you is something I've always envied about you and Mac."

He felt her arms tighten around him.

"I'm sorry about your parents."

Oliver tried not to think about the single mom who'd given him away at the ripe old age of five and put him into a system that generally wanted babies.

He pressed a kiss to the top of Marsali's head and stood there, willing to hold her for as long as she'd let him. "If I'm honest, I think that was one of the things that intrigued me about Mac. The way he'd talk about his family. That first visit, I had to see if it was real."

"Hmm. The truth comes out. You're only dating me for my family."

He squeezed tight. "Brat. Not by a long shot. That was then, this is you. But I will say, as a poor foster kid, it took me a while to like my dorm mate after listening to his homesick stories."

"I remember when Mac first brought *you* home. I was mortified to be caught in my bathing suit. The straggly hair and braces were bad enough but the suit put it over the top."

He chuckled at the memory. "You were beautiful, braces and all. *I* felt like a stray dog being taken in. Probably looked it, too. Now I'm sorry I'm causing issues with you and your family."

She lifted her head from his chest and smiled up at him.

"Are you?"

A smile formed. "To a point," he said and lowered his head for a kiss. "Because I get to do this whenever I want." He kissed her again and squeezed her tight and wished he could soothe the worry he saw in her beautiful eyes. That was something only time could erase. "The interviews are done for today. How are you holding up?"

"Are they all going to ask about our sex life or… lack thereof?"

"Just blush as adorably as you do and let me handle them."

She ducked her head again. "They quoted my book to you about remaining abstinent until committed."

"I know. But at least they didn't try to switch things around and misquote you."

"Wait... How do you know that? You read my dating book for good girls?"

He chuckled low. "I downloaded onto my phone so no one would know what I was reading, but yeah. Of course I did. You wrote it, so I had to read it."

"My own brother didn't read it."

"Maybe if he did he'd be better at dating." A laugh erupted out of her in response to his words, and she lifted her head to stare up at him, a curious frown pinching her eyebrows together. "Come on, what's going on in that beautiful head of yours?"

"Honestly?"

"Always."

"I'm just... going to miss you when you go back to LA tomorrow."

"You could always change your mind and come with me." He'd spent the last several days trying to convince her to join him so he could show her the sights, but so far she'd made excuses. "Come on. You can do your new client interviews online, or have your assistant do them temporarily. Come spend the weekend with me and celebrate the premiere."

"Ollie, I can't. I don't have a dress or the money to spend on the kind of dresses people wear to those things, and you'll be busy schmoozing anyway. I'll just be in the way."

"I'll handle the dress thing. That's not a legitimate excuse."

"I can't let you buy me clothes."

"Why not? It's something I'd love to do for you. Consider it a gift." A thought came to mind. "Didn't you say in your book that women needed to graciously accept the gifts men give them and stop worrying about whether or not acceptance meant giving up their independence? Something about it being face value and just a nice thing to do?"

"I referenced flowers, or the man paying for dinner."

"Yeah, well, this is me, paying for dinner," he said softly. "I don't want to take anything from you, Marsali, only give. And it's Valentine's Day weekend. I don't want to spend it apart. Please, will you come with me?"

She closed her eyes, and while he stared down at her, he could see the war raging in the varied expressions flickering over her face.

"I'd have to find someone to watch Ginger."

"I'll do it for you. I'll help you pack. I'll do whatever you need me to do. Just say yes."

Her teeth sank into her full lower lip, and he

smoothed his thumb over the puffiness, taking in her eyes, the freckles he adored, and the wariness he still sensed in her.

"I… suppose we should spend Valentine's Day together."

"Yes, we should. It would be the best gift you could give me."

"Yeah?"

"Without a doubt."

"I don't want to leave Ginger with strangers. Eliza would but she's playing catch up after being on her honeymoon. I wonder if Mac would watch her?"

"I'll beg him if I have to." Oliver bent his knees and ducked his head to better see her face. "So is that a yes?"

"I… suppose I could reschedule a few things."

Oliver pressed his lips to hers and celebrated the news with a kiss that left them both heavy-eyed and struggling to catch their breath. "Leave it to me. Ginger, the travel arrangements, everything."

"Really?"

"Marsali the matchmaker, you are about to see how Valentine's Day is done."

Chapter 13

Marsali wasn't sure what to expect when they got to LAX the following day, but the security detail awaiting them to help them navigate the crowd who seemed to zero in on them and immediately turn manic wasn't it. People of all ages held up phones, and women as well as girls screamed Oliver's name.

Marsali's heart pounded hard in her chest, so much so she got a little light-headed as they were quickly ushered through the airport to a waiting limo. Oliver kept her close to his side through it all, but once the limo door shut, he turned his back to the window and the faces outside to check on her.

"You okay?"

"Is it always like that?" She watched as Oliver's head bobbed this way and that.

"Sometimes."

"Don't let him kid you. Yes, it's always like that, and thank God, right, Oliver?"

For the first time since entering the limo, Marsali realized they weren't alone. "Oh, my gosh."

The woman's expression changed to one of knowing smugness.

"Evangeline Lorey," she said with her super-sultry voice. "And you're the little secret my dear Oliver has been keeping from us."

"Uh, Marsali… Jones." Marsali glanced at Oliver and found him staring at his co-star with a narrowed gaze.

"What are you doing here, Eva?" Oliver asked.

Marsali blinked at his tone. Not because it was mean or curt but… cautious?

"I wanted to surprise you. Rikki mentioned you were bringing your little friend with you to attend the premiere and that a shopping spree was in order, so I volunteered my services, of course. We can't have your friend's little sister showing up at the premiere looking out of sorts."

"I told Rikki I'd handle it."

Handle it? What was she, a hot biscuit to be tossed across a table? "I can do my own shopping," Marsali said, unable to keep the upset and embarrassment out of her voice no matter how much she tried.

"Oh, no. Time is ticking and we *have* to get you up to speed," Evangeline said. "Oliver, leave the shopping to us girls. Right, Sally?"

"Marsali."

"Oh, yes. Right. Sorry."

"Thanks, Eva, but we don't need your help. I'm taking Marsali myself," Oliver said firmly. "It's part of our special weekend."

Marsali forced a smile at his words, and even though Oliver's statement about their special weekend made her feel a little better, she hated being discussed like a problem instead of a guest.

"I'll join you then. Trust me, you'll want a woman's opinion," Evangeline said to Marsali. "There's a reason men in Hollywood have stylists. Right, Oliver?"

He had a stylist? Really? Maybe she shouldn't have been surprised, but it was yet another thing she didn't know about him after their many years of short, random visits.

"Only because Rikki insists upon it. Part of the image thing Hollywood likes," he said to Marsali.

"Of course it is. You're not shopping discount stores anymore, right?"

The other woman smiled as her gaze lowered and took in Marsali's traveling clothes of discount-store skinny jeans, booties, and flowy blouse topped by a cute jacket. The outfit was perfectly fine for a day out and about in Wilmington or Carolina Cove, but sitting across from the glamorous actress in an outfit that probably cost more than Marsali made in a year, she felt like Cinderella before some heavy-duty fairy dust.

Silence filled the limo as the driver shot them into the LA traffic, and Marsali found her attention split between the scenery, such as it was outside, and the woman giving her a competitive sizing up whenever Oliver wasn't looking.

"So— I'm sorry, *what* was your name again?"

"Marsali," she said, a smile pinned to her face.

"Yes, yes, Marsali. It's so kind of Oliver to treat you to this experience. I mean, I imagine it's not every day a girl like you gets to do something like this."

"Mmm. It is… exciting," Marsali said.

"Of course. It's just there's a lot riding on this premiere, and we wouldn't want anything to over-shadow it or… take away from the evening."

"Eva," Oliver said, his tone a low warning.

"I understand. I'll keep my brightness to a minimum and try not to trip," Marsali said.

"Oh, she has claws," Eva said, smiling. "You *do* like a woman with claws, don't you, *Ollie*?"

Marsali felt Oliver stiffen on the seat beside her, and even though she was getting the vibe that Oliver and the actress were more than costars, she let her hand shift in a show of support for him. Marsali squeezed his leg above his knee and Oliver's hand immediately swallowed hers and held.

"Ah. So sweet."

Oliver cleared his throat. "Eva, Marsali and I can handle the shopping on our own, and since it's one of the few things I've been looking forward to this weekend, I'm going to have Sam drop you off at your hotel."

"Oh, now. What fun is that?"

"I insist," Oliver said. "I want to spend as much time with Marsali as I can before the chaos of the premiere hits. I'm sure you understand."

A long pause followed his words but finally the beautiful actress shrugged.

"Of course. I'm sure I'll see you again when you drop Marsali off later," Evangeline said.

"What do you mean?" Oliver asked.

"Rikki didn't tell you? Marsali and I are both staying at the hotel."

"I see."

She and Oliver hadn't exactly discussed logistics for this trip, but Oliver had told her he had plenty of bedrooms and Marsali had just assumed she'd be staying in one of them. "There's no need to go to the expense. I-I can stay at Oliver's in one of his spare rooms." It wasn't ideal but she hated that he was spending so much on her.

"No, she's right," Oliver murmured, his tone regretful. "It's… best, all things considered."

"Now, now, no fighting. Surely you understand our Oliver here is no saint," Eva added with a salacious grin. "We wouldn't want your precious reputation getting sullied."

Sullied? Marsali was well aware that Eva mocked her, but she'd thought Oliver would—

Oliver's hand squeezed hers tight but he didn't respond to Eva's comments. Marsali tried and failed not to be hurt by his lack of defense.

"Sam? We're dropping Eva back off at her hotel."

"Yes, sir, Mr. Beck."

The woman's eyes narrowed on Marsali and she

felt the malice being glared her way. Oliver's costar was yet another frenemy.

And Marsali had a feeling the fun had only started.

TWO HOURS after touching down in LAX, Marsali found herself in one of LA's posh boutiques. The saleswoman eyed Oliver with a salacious expression and gave Marsali a look that made it clear that she wondered what he found in her. Still, she loaded up with gowns and ushered Marsali to a changing room that was larger than her dining room in Carolina Cove.

Marsali eyed the array of colorful gowns. Even she knew buying off the rack wasn't done for events such as this, but given the lack of time, it would have to do. That and the fact Marsali refused to allow Oliver to spend any more money than absolutely necessary. Maybe she could find something reasonably affordable that she could pay back in time? The dress, hotel, and whatever else he had planned were quickly adding up. Some women might like that kind of money being spent on them, but it put Marsali on edge after Oliver's lack of defense earlier.

A glance at the price tags left her gasping and she barely held in a moan. Okay, then. No new car for her anytime soon. Because unless something happened to change her mind, she *would* be paying Oliver back.

The first gown was a deep purple with a plunging neckline. Marsali barely dared to breathe as she exited the dressing room and found Oliver sitting in a plush and buttoned chair drinking a glass of champagne. The sales clerk hovered nearby but Marsali was only aware of Oliver as his gaze shifted and swept over her body. After a long moment, he shook his head and she breathed a sigh of relief.

"Beautiful, but no."

The second had a high neck, but the backless gown gathered just at her hips, and one wrong move made her think it would wind up on a meme somewhere. Another no, for which she was eternally grateful.

Gown three was a high-low gown that couldn't seem to make up its mind given the lace and tulle and satin and silk and buttons. She refused to leave the dressing room and went on to number four, much to Oliver's amusement.

Number four wasn't much better. The gown fit

well, but even she knew the color wasn't right for her. Oliver's squinting look confirmed it, and back into the room she went again.

Shopping was normally fun and something she enjoyed, but this was already losing its luster.

Maybe she'd like it better if the clerk wasn't quite so attentive to Oliver and could care less about helping her now that she was out of the way and struggling with the gowns.

Marsali flipped through the many items hanging in the room staged for her, dismissing one after another until she finally uncovered one in the back. Plain. Simple. Elegant. It lacked the flash of the glitzy, glamorous gowns but made Marsali think of old romantic movies.

Getting into the ball gown on her own took some doing, but the moment Marsali turned to face the overly ornate dressing mirror, she knew this was the gown she wanted, no matter what the salesclerk, Oliver, or Hollywood might say or think.

"Hey, how you doing in there?" Oliver asked from the other side of the door.

"I… I found one. I want it."

"Can I see?"

She continued to stare at her reflection and shook her head. "No."

A short pause followed.

"Okay, then," he said, amusement clear in his voice. "Change and the clerk will get it ready. Marsali?"

"Yeah?"

"I can't wait to see you in it."

She bit her lip and took a breath, hoping the gown had the impact on him that it did for her.

Back in her street clothes, she handed the gown over to the clerk, who raised an eyebrow at her choice when compared to the others but didn't comment other than to say she would prep it for delivery to the hotel.

Shoes were next, and since the gown was floor-length and covered her feet, she chose low heels and a blinged-out clutch for a bit of splash.

"Don't forget jewelry," Oliver said.

"Oh, no. Oliver, I couldn't possibly."

"Most times people rent the jewelry, dear," the clerk behind the counter informed her.

The woman was older, with kinder eyes and a visibly gentler disposition. "Oh. I see. Um…"

"What do you recommend?" Oliver asked, moving to stand behind Marsali.

"Well, with that gown"—the clerk glanced at the

rows of displays beneath the glass—"perhaps these earrings and… this."

Marsali was confused because of the necklace the woman had chosen. "Oh, um, I'm not sure how that would work. Perhaps you're thinking of a different gown?" She glanced at Oliver, and he winked at her as though he could tell she was getting overwhelmed by all the fuss.

"Ah, I heard it's a surprise," the woman said. "May I?"

She motioned for Marsali to step close and whispered instructions, and Marsali couldn't help but think the woman was a genius because she would never have thought of it. "Yeah, that… It would be perfect," Marsali said, exchanging a smile with the woman. "Thank you."

"My pleasure, dear. And may I say you two make a lovely couple. Enjoy your wonderful evening. She will be riveting," the woman said to Oliver.

"She already is," Oliver said. "Are we all done here?"

"I think so. Are we going to your house now or the hotel…?"

His low chuckle sounded in her ear as he kissed her cheek. "Sweetheart, we're just getting started."

Chapter 14

Marsali was exhausted by the time they made it to Oliver's home in Beverly Hills, which was, by Hollywood's standards, quite modest despite it being thirty-five-hundred square feet of beautifully designed space.

"You're awfully quiet. You don't like it?" he asked.

She turned from the windows looking out to a gorgeously landscaped pool, hot tub, and outdoor kitchen and eating area to face Oliver and found him moving toward her. She welcomed him with open arms, more than ready to rest her head on his broad chest. "It's beautiful as I'm sure you already know. It suits you, actually."

"You sound surprised."

She couldn't stop the smile from forming. "I guess I expected something less homey."

And homey was an apt description. The house had four gorgeously appointed bedrooms, each with its own equally decadent bath with either a deep tub or massive shower or both. During the quick tour, she'd noted his penchant for massive shower heads in the ceilings, and she found herself wishing she could forego the hotel stay and sleep here just to experience one of those showers firsthand.

Well, and to be closer to Oliver. She didn't like the idea of being so far away from him in a strange city with people—the women especially—circling like sharks.

But realistically she knew, for her family's sake, her brand's sake, and the morals that convicted her, that Oliver was right. She might not be a world-famous star, but she had built a certain following, and that following expected her to adhere to the standards she'd created for herself in the last eight years. She had to set an example rather than talk about it to her clients and readers.

"Ready to see the rest?" he asked.

The kitchen and living room of Oliver's home

were just as inviting and beautiful, the colors masculine with its gray walls, black cabinets, and sleek gray and white countertops with a waterfall island. Overall the look was clean and uncluttered. Perfect for a busy bachelor.

"When I got to the point I could buy something, the only thing I could think of was that I wanted a sanctuary. Someplace I could truly relax and get away from the crazy. I found the cheapest house in the nicest neighborhood and made it a project."

She blinked at his words. "You mean you remodeled and decorated it and stuff?"

"I had help, trust me. But, yeah. I wanted it to be the home I never had and always wanted. And once I'm inside and those doors close, no one can see me unless I want them to."

He lowered his head and pressed a kiss to her lips.

"You hungry?"

"Hmm," she said, wrinkling her nose. "If I'm going to the premier, I shouldn't eat. That dress fit like a glove."

He kissed her again and lingered.

"I can't wait to see it. Though it feels a bit like I'm taking you to prom. Did I ever tell you how jealous I got the night of your senior prom when that guy… What was his name?"

"Uh, Peter?"

"Yeah, Peeping Peter."

"What? Why did you call him that?"

"Because we caught him and one of his buddies spying on you the following day when you were in the pool. I don't know which one of us was angrier, me or Mac."

"Wait, I thought you hit him because he'd started that rumor about me?"

"What rumor?"

She rolled her eyes and shrugged. "The rumor immature teenage boys start about girls and prom."

"I'm gonna have to look Peter up again," Oliver said, his expression darkening.

"Stop it. I can't believe I didn't realize all these years. I thought the punch was for that. He was such a creep. Who hit him? Tell me."

"Mac. I wound up having to play peacemaker, which did not make me happy."

"Does it make you feel any better that he got teased unmercifully for wearing makeup to school that Monday for pictures?"

"Hmm. Some. And that reminds me, hair and makeup will be here tomorrow at two."

Hair and makeup? "Is that… necessary?" Oliver was pulling out all the stops, but was it so she fit the required image Oliver apparently had to maintain or as part of her Valentine's Day treat? "I mean, thank you, but you've done too much already. I can do my own."

"Uh-huh. They'll be here at two, right after lunch and a couples massage."

A laugh bubbled up out of her chest. "Oliver— Ollie," she corrected immediately when she saw him open his mouth to protest. "I love the gifts, don't get me wrong, but I know how careful you are with money. I've… heard things from Mac and from you over the years. It's not that I'm not grateful, it's just… you've spoiled me so much already today. The gown and accessories and the after-party clothes."

"Marsali, I've waited a long time for this. For you, *us*. I know it's a lot coming at you all at once, but can you just enjoy the pampering? Because I'm being honest when I tell you I'm enjoying being able to do it for you."

Oh, wow. When he put it that way… "Really?"

"Yes, really."

She inhaled, still torn because, while she loved

the romantic aspects of all he offered, she worried about...

What? That you'll like it too much?

She managed to hold in a groan. Because realistically that was true. She liked the pampering and gifts. Loved the idea of a couples massage and the fact Oliver had seemed to enjoy watching her reactions as she'd tried on the different outfits because he knew it was fun for her. Different.

So focus on the moment. Enjoy the moment.

That's all she had to do, right?

"I was thinking after all the travel and shopping today, we might have a quiet dinner here. Is that okay?"

She squeezed him tighter and reveled in the feel of his strength. "Oh, yes. I was hoping for some quiet, to be honest. I never knew shopping could be so exhausting. I might go jump in that hot tub and not come out."

He laughed and snuggled her closer. "Then do that while I crank up the grill. Steak sound good? Maybe some fresh veggies?"

"Perfect. But I'll help you."

"No. I'd much rather see you in that hot tub."

"My suit is at the hotel, and no, I'm not skinny-dipping."

He looked heartbroken at her comment before grinning at her once more. "There are multiple suits in the pool house. Help yourself."

"You… keep women's bathing suits on hand?"

"I do when it keeps them from using it as an excuse to skinny-dip." He shook his head and made a disgruntled face. "It's for my protection," he said. "I have men's *and* women's suits at all times after one of Rikki's ideas to schmooze some of the producers and directors and moneymen wound up becoming something I can't unsee to this day."

She couldn't imagine having her home overtaken like that. The level of disrespect and… "You were okay with that?"

"No. I actually left and came back the next day. Rikki knows to not plan anything here now, but I still keep suits on hand just in case. I use the pool house mostly as an office now."

Okay, then.

"Marsali, I probably shouldn't have told you that story, because I can see how you're looking at me now, but that life is not me. Never has been. I've dated, I've had fun, yes, but I don't go for that type of party. Do you hear what I'm saying?"

She nodded, relief pouring through her. She'd be so disappointed in him if he had.

"So go help yourself to a suit. They're in the dresser drawers in the bedroom. I'll turn on some music and get the grill going, and let's have a nice night just the two of us. Okay?"

"Sounds perfect."

Oliver released her only to stop her and tug her close to kiss again, lingering until she finally pulled away and shooed him toward the grill.

She made her way to the pool house and entered, thinking about how far Oliver had come in his life. From foster kid to college hunk to movie star.

Marsali changed into the most modest two-piece she could find, which, by Hollywood's standards, wasn't all that modest. For her own sake, she added a cover-up and told herself it was because she would be cold. That done, she piled her hair atop her head in a messy bun and found a towel before checking her appearance one last time.

She moved through the small pool house, taking in more of the details. It really was lovely. Simple. It also had a small kitchen the size of hers back in North Carolina, an eating area with couch and chairs for relaxing in front of a very large television. The bathroom she'd used was attached to a bedroom on one side of the house and on the other side… Oliver's office.

Still, all this room for just one person?

She moved toward the office, and the pictures atop the mantel drew her.

Oliver stood outside at the grill, and she used the opportunity for what it was, a chance to get to know the Hollywood version of him. There were stacks of scripts on a desk, some flagged for him to read right away. There were also stacks of papers, a calendar that looked very full, books on… directing and producing. Oliver wanted to do that? Was interested in the behind-the-scenes stuff?

Apparently so.

She moved on to the shelf across the room and found more books on a wide variety of subjects relating to life in Hollywood. There were also books on business and money management, with a few of her favorites from Dave Ramsey and Chris Hogan.

But photos lined the shelf above the books, and she caught her breath when she recognized the faces that stared back at Oliver whenever he was in this room.

The first photo was of him and Mac, arms draped over each other's shoulders as they smiled at the camera on graduation day. Only weeks before,

Oliver had been contacted by the modeling company and offered an insane amount of money to sign with them.

She realized now what a lure that must have been a to a kid who'd grown up with nothing. And just how tempting it must have been to take the money and walk away from his business major. Not Oliver, though. He'd stuck it out, graduated with honors. Then went for the money.

The next photo was of her family. She cringed at the image of her with her crazy curls and braces but found it sweet that he'd had it framed. That photo had been taken at Easter after church. Oliver had attended with them.

The last…

She gasped. Marsali's hand trembled as she reached out and took the photo in hand. It was the one taken at her parents' anniversary party. The one where she smiled up at him like a lovesick—

"There you are."

She turned to find Oliver standing in the doorway, watching her. His gaze dropped to the frame in her hand.

"That is one of my favorites."

"You framed it?"

"I did."

"But we weren't…"

He shoved himself off of the wood and ambled toward her with lazy steps.

"No, we weren't."

He stared at her a long moment before tilting his head toward the door.

"Dinner will be ready soon."

Dinner. A quiet evening at home. A hot tub. Her heart pounded in her chest.

Her feelings for Oliver grew with every moment, but she wasn't prepared for whatever came next. Did Oliver expect this trip to be more?

Did… she?

DINNER WAS DELICIOUS, the wine the best he could find in his collection. The view of Marsali in his hot tub—

Yeah, he needed to make that a normal occurrence. Figure out a way to convince her Hollywood wasn't as bad as she seemed to think and maybe she should consider moving her business to a more lucrative side of the country.

But how?

He was ready and willing to walk her to the altar right now, but he had a feeling she'd run in the opposite direction due to the speed. Especially the way she'd eyed him when he'd joined her in the hot tub.

But the sight of her in that bathing suit… He'd thought his head might explode, and he thanked God that no one else was around to see her like that except for him. The beautiful image was now imprinted in his head for all eternity.

Three hours later, Oliver walked Marsali to her hotel room, wishing all the while she could've stayed under the same roof. Maybe it was best Rikki had set it up this way, though, because the more time he spent with her, the more willing he was to forego common sense and just let things play out however they would. It was nobody's business what they did or didn't do. Right?

But protecting Marsali from that kind of press had to be a priority. There were women… and then there were women like Marsali, who made the effort of courtship worth all the fuss. She was one in a million and he didn't want to screw it up.

He felt the tension in her grow as they walked toward her room. They'd talked in the tub, shared some kisses and cuddles, but when things had started to heat up, she'd pulled away. And he under-stood why.

Marsali believed in what she wrote, and he believed in her. He was willing to sacrifice his desires for her well-being. Their well-being. Especially when it could mean a future together. One that would last because it was born in friendship and respect.

He caught her arm just before they got to her door and tugged her toward him.

"Ollie…"

He kissed her quiet, lingering over the contact. "I had fun today. I hope you did, too."

"I did. So much. Thank you."

"You're welcome. Good night, Marsali."

She blinked up at him, eyes wide with surprise. A low laugh left his chest. "You're worth the wait, sweetheart. Besides, tomorrow is going to be a longer day than today, and once the premiere is behind us, I plan on showing you around. You need to sleep while you can."

She hesitated a long moment, just staring at him, then rose to her tiptoes with her hand against his chest for balance and kissed him again, this kiss longer and sweeter and full of the promise of more.

"Thank you for understanding me."

He kissed her again, unable to leave her just yet.

"Marsali?" he said softly once the kiss had ended and she'd twisted the knob to enter her room.

"What?"

"That doesn't mean I won't be dreaming about us."

Color rushed to her cheeks and Oliver chuckled as he turned away.

Chapter 15

Marsali opened her heavy-lidded eyes the next morning and stared across at Oliver, facedown on the massage table next to her.

The day had started off with breakfast at the hotel before he'd whisked her off in the limo back to his house, where she'd met his agent, Rikki. The woman had looked Marsali up and down during the introduction, and once again, Marsali felt as though she'd come up lacking in the girlfriend department.

Would that ever change? Granted, she knew perceptions of movie stars were skewed all over the spectrum, but she wasn't chopped liver. She had a successful business, had written a bestselling book. Yeah, not chopped liver!

Oliver's agent had pinned a smile on her very plumped lips and asked to speak to Oliver in private.

She wasn't sure what Rikki had discussed with Oliver, but an hour later, Rikki was somewhere in the house while she and Oliver enjoyed fabulous massages that made Marsali aware of every nerve ending in her body.

"Relax, miss. Today is a fun day, no?" the masseuse said to her in a thick German accent.

The woman's question caused Oliver to lift his head from the rest, and Marsali managed to smile at him. "Yes, it's a fun day. I'm just nervous."

Because anyone in their right mind would be. Especially someone like her. All eyes would be on Oliver, and the thought of standing at his side was, well, *daunting*.

"It's going to be fun," Oliver said from the bed across from her. "Stop worrying."

"Did, um, Rikki say anything about you bringing me tonight?"

Had she not been watching him, she wouldn't have noticed the way he tensed at the question.

"She mentioned it."

Really? That was it? All he was going to say? "She'd rather you took someone else."

Oliver shifted on the bed and the masseuse immediately took a step back as Oliver rose to sit on the table facing her.

"Why are you worrying about this stuff, Marsali?"

This stuff? "It's..." She glanced at his masseuse and wondered how much she should say in front of them. "I know I'm the outsider here."

"No, you're not. Not when you're going with me. Got it?"

She nodded and had to close her eyes and hold her breath when her masseuse ran her knuckles from her shoulders up her neck to her ears and pressed.

"Mmm," Oliver murmured. "The look on your face."

She opened her eyes in time to see him brace his hands on the side of the table over the sheet, trapping her arms beneath, and bend to capture her lips, ignoring the women in the room.

The kiss didn't last long, but Marsali's face flooded with heat when he lifted his head and stared into her eyes. The look he gave her... Her toes curled and she struggled to take a normal breath.

"I'm going to go shower. Don't forget makeup and hair will be here in forty-five minutes or so."

Once Oliver had left the room, Marsali's massage person did a few more strokes to try to release the tension now back in her shoulders.

"All done, miss. Sit up slowly in case you're light-headed."

Marsali laughed. Light-headed? Oh, yeah, she was, but it had nothing to do with the massage and everything to do with Oliver Beck.

SEVERAL HOURS LATER, Marsali sat in the chair, facing away from the mirror, and wondered if the torture was ever going to end. Was she that much of a mess?

Once dried, her hair had been loosely pulled back from her face into a neat, low chignon that showcased her curls without giving them free rein. The look was soft and sexy, and one she'd have to try to mimic in the future.

The makeup artist had gone next, and after so much time in the chair, Marsali was anxious to see the results.

Finally the woman deemed her finished and slowly twisted the chair around to face the mirror. Marsali blinked, unsure of who stared back at her. Her eyes were huge, dark, and smoky. Her lips full and pouty. Her skin smooth and perfect to the point she was afraid to smile for fear of cracking the facade caked on her face.

A soft knock sounded on the door.

"Perfect timing," the makeup artist, Dianne, said. "Come in."

Oliver entered and stopped in his tracks. Marsali met his gaze in the mirror and waited for his reaction. "What... do you think?" she asked after the long pause.

Oliver glanced at the makeup artist, who also waited expectantly before meeting Marsali's gaze once more. "You look beautiful but..."

But?

"It's not you."

Marsali wasn't sure who gasped the loudest, her or Dianne. "You don't like it?"

Oliver stalked toward them and knelt on the floor in front of Marsali.

"Mr. Beck, Rikki was quite clear in her instructions to—"

"Rikki doesn't get to dictate Marsali's makeup," Oliver said.

He glanced at the makeup artist and then the cart she'd wheeled in with her when she'd arrived.

Oliver grabbed a box from the bottom and flipped the lid, earning another gasp from the woman.

"Oh, Mr. Beck—"

He held up the makeup wipe.

"Marsali, do you like it?"

"It's… a bit much. I don't look like myself."

He held out the wipe for her to take, and she bit her lip, glancing up at Dianne because she didn't want to hurt the woman's feelings.

Oliver seemed to understand her hesitation, because he leaned forward and swiped the wet cloth across her cheek, earning a loud moan from the woman.

"Dianne, Marsali has the most gorgeous freckles I've ever seen. They're sweet and *insanely* sexy, and I can't see a one of them," Oliver murmured. He tossed the first towel in the trash and pulled another from the box, gently swiping it across her other cheek and then her nose. "She is naturally beautiful and needs very little foundation."

"I… understand, Mr. Beck. I'll keep her as natural as possible."

Marsali stared at him, tears in her eyes because… this was her Ollie, protecting her, looking out for her. Her heart broke open a bit more, the crack filling with more love because he understood her so well and knew she hated being caked with makeup and unable to even touch her face for fear of leaving a streak behind.

Oliver continued to wash her face but left the eye shadow on her eyes. When he finished, her freckles and face were bare.

Marsali looked in the mirror once more and swallowed hard, her attention shifting to the doorway behind her when movement caught her notice.

Rikki stood watching, listening, an indiscernible expression on her very Hollywood-esque face while Oliver thanked the makeup artist for her willingness to start over.

Marsali watched as Rikki stepped back into the hallway and disappeared. Marsali sighed, her stomach taut, because in that moment, however innocently, she knew she'd made another frenemy.

Chapter 16

Oliver was in the process of pulling on his tuxedo shirt when Rikki barged into his bedroom minutes later. "Seriously? You ever hear of knocking?"

"Oh, please, like I haven't seen it before. Besides, what did you expect after that stunt earlier?"

"What stunt?"

"You do realize how important it is to maintain the right image, don't you? I mean, it's only been the *one thing* I've been working to achieve for you these last *ten* years."

"What does Marsali's makeup have to do with my image?"

"More than you'd think. Not to mention the fact that you undermined me. Again."

He yanked on the edges of his shirt and focused on fastening the buttons. "Yeah, well, I don't agree with some of your dictates. You're my agent, but that doesn't give you total control over my life—or someone I date. Especially micro-managing something like her makeup."

"Actually, it does. What did I tell you from the beginning? If you want to succeed in Hollywood, you do what I say, when I say, and you trust that it's for your best. Whoever you date? It's expected they fit the image we've worked so hard to achieve."

He finished fastening most of the buttons and went to work on the sleeves. "When you took me on as a kid fresh out of college, I needed that kind of help, but that isn't the case now. I think I've more than proven myself—and learned quite a bit in the process."

Rikki's lips pursed and she glared at him.

"We've come too far for you to let some girl mess with the plan."

Anger filled him and he struggled to maintain his cool. "Marsali isn't just some girl."

"No, no, no," Rikki said, closing her eyes as she rolled her head back on her neck. "Do you *hear* yourself? Where is my superstar? My marketable bachelor? Hollywood's *hottest*? What are you doing right now?"

"I'm living my life. What good is it to work as hard as I do if I'm not allowed to enjoy the fruits of it? Be with who I want to be with?"

Rikki's expression soured even more.

"Your career is still on the upswing, Oliver, but a large part of that is because of your single status and the very careful plan I put into place to get you where *we* agreed you have the potential to go. That hometown girl in there is *not* part of that plan."

"That's where you're wrong. She's been a part of my life all along. You just haven't kept up to speed."

"You're letting sentiment get the best of you. You can do so much better, Oliver. What about Eva? Her career is as hot as yours. You look delicious together. You two are *made* for each—"

Rikki broke off abruptly and Oliver turned to find Marsali standing in the open doorway to his bedroom.

The air left his lungs in a rush due to the expression on her face. How long had she been there?

Too long.

"Rikki, we're done here."

"Oliver—"

"You need to go get ready for tonight." He turned to look at his agent and wondered if his frustration with her was simply coming to a head after a year or so of building or if it had to do with Rikki's comments on Marsali alone. Either way, he wanted her gone.

"Fine. I'll see you there," Rikki said as she brushed by Marsali without a word and stalked out the door on her four-inch heels.

Oliver moved toward Marsali, stopping when he stood bare toes to her slippered feet. The makeup artist had outdone herself this time. Marsali's freckles were visible, her eyes looked huge and even more beautiful, and her lips invited thoughts he struggled to control. "Wow."

Marsali tilted her head to one side as she stared up at him.

"I take it you approve this time?"

"You looked amazing before, don't get me wrong. But now? You take my breath away. The only problem is I want to kiss you and I can't or I'll muss you."

Marsali was quiet a moment, and Oliver could see the wheels cranking behind her eyes and knew

Rikki was the source. "Marsali, whatever you heard, ignore it. Please?"

"That's kind of hard to do when your agent doesn't like me. Or that I'm here."

He knew platitudes wouldn't cut it and decided to be straightforward. "This is my life, not hers."

"But if I'm bad for your career…"

"Ignore everything she said. I mean it. Rikki and I haven't been seeing eye to eye on a lot of things lately. She's overstepping on a multitude of levels she doesn't get a say in."

"If you say so."

"I do." His gaze lowered to take in the robe she wore. "You wearing that to the premiere?"

She lifted a perfectly groomed eyebrow high and smiled. "It's awfully comfortable. What would you say if I did?"

"I say we start a new trend."

"Ah, I bet Rikki would have *lots* to say about that. Actually, I came to make sure I passed the test before I got into my gown."

"There is no test, sweetheart. Do you feel more comfortable?"

She wrinkled her nose, a wry expression flick-ering over her face.

"The makeup earlier was… a lot. This is definitely better."

He ran his knuckles lightly over her cheek, his gaze following. "You have no idea how much I want to kiss every freckle you have. I didn't like not being able to see them."

As he knew it would, her face flushed with rosy color and he grinned, loving that he could elicit that kind of immediate response from her.

"I-I should go get dressed."

"Is Dianne still here?"

"Yes. She's waiting for me to come back with the okay before she leaves."

"Good," he said. "That means she can fix your lipstick when I'm done."

MANY HOURS LATER, Marsali was in the ladies' room wondering how women in the old days ever managed to go to the bathroom when it meant battling yards of material.

Still, she'd never forget the moment when she'd appeared in the living room earlier. She'd known the gown was flattering but doubts had still crept in—until she'd seen Oliver's face. If he'd told her once how beautiful, stunning, and sexy she looked, he'd told her a dozen times.

And the long necklace worn backwards with its teardrop diamond dangling down her back had prompted a murmur of how he'd have to buy the piece just to see her wear it and nothing else. Her face had exploded with color, earning a low chuckle from him. But in that moment, she'd wanted the same thing, to have that intimacy with Oliver and a future and kids and all of the romance possible when two people just got each other.

The premiere had gone well. They'd arrived to a slew of camera flashes and screams and requests for photos, and Oliver had kept a firm hold of her waist so that she couldn't escape the attention being lavished on them. He'd even made a show of kissing her when requested, though the kiss was light and careful of her lipstick, unlike before.

But all the while, Marsali was aware that Rikki had stood nearby, looking super sexy in a bright red gown that was everything Marsali's wasn't.

Eva was there as well. The actress had chosen a super-short gown in dark plum that showcased her long legs in high stilettos, and with her straight dark hair and perfect face, Marsali could see why Rikki and anyone would think Eva and Oliver to be well paired. Their height, gorgeous looks, and similar careers would be enough to make Marsali believe they'd share enough commonalities that could easily form a power couple.

Marsali left the bathroom stall and washed her hands before opening her bag to reapply the lip stain and gloss the makeup artist had given her. The bathroom door opened and Eva appeared as though conjured by her thoughts.

The woman moved to the mirrors where Marsali stood and removed a small compact.

"Eva, you were great in the movie. I totally bought you as a forensic scientist." Kill 'em with kindness. That's what her dad had always said.

The woman gave Marsali a slight smile and turned, leaning against the counter. She crossed one ankle over the other, and the pose left Marsali feeling short and frumpy in her layers of gown.

"What are you doing?"

"Pardon?" Marsali asked.

"With Oliver. What are you doing? Do you really think you can have something with him? Fit into his life?"

Marsali stiffened, surprised by the woman's direct attack. "I don't see how it's any of your busi-ness. And Oliver and I have been friends a very long time."

"Not what I asked. But that statement is just more proof you're using him to better your career."

"Eva—"

"You have *nothing* to offer him. Nothing that can help him. The only thing you're going to do is hold him back."

"Considering Oliver is a smart, successful actor, I don't see how that's possible—or any of your concern."

"Oh, but it is," Evangeline said as she turned to leave. "Oliver is very much my concern."

Evangeline left and Marsali pressed her hand to her stomach to fight off the wave of nerves and anxiety bombarding her.

The way Eva had made her parting comment… Maybe Eva and Oliver had been something more than costars, but that was the past, right? She couldn't hold the past against him so long as that relationship was over.

But the last thing she'd ever want to do was hurt Oliver or damage his career, and she'd seen the way everyone looked at her tonight. The curiosity, the judgment. Eva was right about that. People found her lacking, and even though she was a big girl and knew not to let their opinions bother her, they did. How could they not?

No one wanted to be where they weren't welcome.

She made her way out of the ladies' room and snagged a glass of champagne from a strolling waiter. Across the room, Eva and Oliver posed for photos, looking very chic and gorgeous together, just like they had in the movie when they were running from bad guys and sharing heated, rip-their-clothes-off scenes before the screen faded to black. Had those scenes carried over to real life? Was that why Eva and Rikki were both so upset by her presence?

As she stood watching Oliver with Eva, Marsali noticed something about them. The… familiarity. She supposed after filming together for months it was natural but… Now she wondered and jealousy stabbed hard.

Marsali watched Eva cozy up to Oliver. His arm was around her tiny waist in a perfectly respectable place, but Eva had an arm around his waist and another tucked at his chest.

The air left Marsali's lungs in a gush that sounded way too loud. Thankfully no one stood close enough to hear. She turned away from the sight of them, unable to cope with the gut-wrenching awareness settling deep within her at the pose and what it suggested.

This was Hollywood. Sex was as common as people changing clothes. Oliver had a life before her on-air blunder, and he had a life and career that involved kissing gorgeous, half-naked women.

The question that remained… could she handle watching it happen?

Chapter 17

Valentine's Day. Oliver couldn't remember the last time he'd actually had a significant other on Valentine's Day, which was why he might have gone a little overboard. He smiled because it wouldn't be the last.

"Where are we going?" she asked.

"I thought you liked surprises."

"I do but you can't blame me for being curious."

He glanced across the interior of his tricked-out Jeep, loving the look of her with the wind in her hair and her freckles calling to him.

The premiere had gone well but it had been a long night. And after way too many hours of posing for the camera, doing interviews, and schmoozing with those who could make or break his career with a single phone call, he'd sensed a growing tension in Marsali that hadn't abated.

The after-party was held in the ballroom of Marsali's hotel—another bit of Rikki's careful planning he'd bet—and several hours in, Marsali had excused herself, citing jet lag. Leaving her at her hotel room door last night had been difficult, but he'd managed, all the while wondering how he could convince her to cancel her flight back to North Carolina and stay with him. He hadn't wanted to return to the party afterward, not without Marsali at his side.

"So, where are we going again?" Marsali asked for the tenth time.

He reached over and grasped her hand in his, lifting it to his lips to kiss. "I asked a favor from a friend. Did you enjoy last night? You left kind of early."

Marsali shifted toward him on the seat. "You needed some time without me. But, yeah, I enjoyed it. It was fun getting dressed up, though I think my dress wasn't the norm."

"You were gorgeous. It was perfect."

"I forgot to tell you that the movie was okay."

He glanced at her to find her shooting him an ornery grin. "Brat."

"Hey, last night was plenty of proof that you do not need me feeding your ego. You have way too many minions for that."

Oliver shook his head, knowing she was right and appreciating the fact that she was a straight shooter. "True enough."

"Oh. Wow."

He smiled when he realized Marsali hadn't been paying attention and was only now aware they'd made it to the 101. The Pacific Ocean stretched out to his left but his focus was on the road and Marsali.

"That is so *beautiful*."

He smiled at her and cranked up the radio. With the top pushed back on the Jeep and tunes blasting, he drove them toward Malibu.

They made a few stops along the way, pulling into spots for photo ops and shops he was familiar with. Finally they reached their destination, and he grabbed the picnic basket he'd snuck into the Jeep while she'd tried on hats to help control her curls in the wind.

"That was not there when we left this morning."

He grinned at her excitement. "I called ahead and got it while you were distracted. Grab that blanket."

"You've thought of everything."

"Hey, I'm romancing a matchmaker. I have to bring my A-game."

"I don't know. Rikki and Eva would argue that need. They say we're… too different."

"They said that to you? When?" Anger filled him, and even though he knew Rikki was upset, he couldn't believe Eva had jumped into the fray.

"It doesn't matter."

"It does." He wrapped his arm around her neck and tugged her close for a kiss. "Because they're wrong. You hear me?"

MARSALI STILL BATTLED her thoughts as she leaned back against Oliver's chest a while later and stared at the waves coming in. He couldn't have planned a better date for them. And with hats and sunglasses and hoodies, they blended in with the others on the beach just enjoying the day.

"What are you thinking about?"

She turned her head into the press of his lips. They landed at her temple. "Just wishing we could stay in the bubble. I saw that frown on your face when you checked messages earlier. Bad news?"

"No. Good news. As soon as we get back, I have to take a look at a script and make a decision soon about a role. Rikki's been negotiating terms, and I guess the production company isn't giving her any problems."

She leaned her head back and stared up at him. "Did you ever think when you were a kid that you'd be where you are now?"

His arms tightened around her and he nuzzled her neck.

"I never thought I'd be here with you. And I am so glad I am."

Sweet. Oliver always said something sweet, and each and every time, her heart cracked open a bit more despite the fear wanting to snap it shut. "Me, either. Is it… weird for you?"

"Not at all. You?"

She bit her lower lip and shook her head, because when she was with him like this, it seemed like the most natural thing in the world. Wasn't that all that mattered? "So tell me about this part."

"I don't know much about it. Supposed to be big, though. Best move I can make, according to Rikki."

"Where, um, will you be filming?"

He chuckled softly. "Can't tell you that either. Rikki let me know the script was delivered after we left today, so it's waiting on me to look over. The production company wants to start filming right away, though."

With his words, the bubble burst. Her job, her life, and family, were in Wilmington, and who knew where Oliver would wind up filming. It meant the upcoming weeks would be spent apart, and even though they'd only just gotten together in the last few weeks, it wasn't something she looked forward to. Relationships were hard enough without tossing distance into the mix.

"If I do it, would you fly in? Work remotely from the site?"

She grimaced at the question. In theory, yes, she could. But she'd always found she got a better feel for her clients when she did the interviews in person. Video interviews were definitely a second choice because it was harder to read body language and expressions that way. "I don't know. Maybe."

"Well, there's time to figure things out. I haven't said yes yet."

"But Rikki wants you to do it?"

"Yeah. It's a series and really high-profile, so the work is good, the pay is off the charts, and it's the next step for me right now. Something I haven't done before."

Oliver stood and held out his hand, tugging her

to her feet before cradling her face in his palms to kiss her. It was a long time before he let her up for air but when he did, Marsali inhaled a shaky breath. There was nothing like Oliver's kisses.

But she couldn't help but wonder… how many of his costars felt the same way?

Chapter 18

It was early evening when they made it back to Oliver's home in Beverly Hills, and after a trip to the restroom to freshen up, Marsali made her way through the house to find Oliver, who sat outside in the sun, opening a package.

As she walked toward him, she saw him toss several books onto the table in front of him to focus on the papers he removed next. The script? Or the contract? She wasn't sure how things worked here in that regard.

She paused inside the house, taking in Oliver as he lowered himself onto one of the cushioned seats and flipped the cover of the bundled papers to begin reading. It seemed surreal to her how they'd managed to get to this point in their friendship-turned-relationship in such a short amount of time. But she loved seeing him look so relaxed and at ease as he reviewed whatever came next for him.

Oliver must have felt her perusal, because he lifted his head, his gaze zeroing in on her.

"Hey, beautiful. You going to join me?"

She lowered her arms to her sides and stepped out of the house. "You look very nice sitting there, Mr. Beck."

He grinned at her words and motioned for her to sit beside him, but when she got close, he tugged her down on his lap.

"You look very nice no matter what."

Oliver used his hold to bring her head low for a kiss. As it always did whenever he touched her, Marsali's mind whirled and heat unfurled deep inside of her. "Mmm," she said, ending the kiss and snuggling against him. She burrowed her face into his neck and inhaled, loving the scent of his cologne and sea air and that indefinable something that was just Oliver. "So what's the initial verdict?" she asked. "Any idea where they'll be filming?"

"Looks like the story is set in Paris."

Paris? Paris, France? *That's one heck of a remote location.* "Oh. Wow. Okay, I guess I won't be seeing you for a while."

"Oh, yeah? Think you're going to get rid of me that easily?"

Oliver began tickling her playfully and she scrambled to get away from him. As she landed on the cushion beside Oliver, her foot hit the coffee table and knocked the stack of three books to the patio floor. "Oh! Sorry."

Oliver's husky chuckles filled her ear as he took advantage of her almost prone position, nibbling her ear. Her gaze locked on the covers of the books near her and she froze, despite the tingling teasing Oliver continued to lavish on her neck. "Um, Oliver?"

"Mmm?"

"What are those?"

He raised his head, a bemused expression on his face.

"What are what?"

"The books?"

"Oh," he said, moving back to kiss her neck. "They sent the book series and the first script."

Her body went hot and cold in an instant. "That's the series they want you for? You'd be the male lead?"

The throatiness of her tone must have gotten through to him, because he lifted his head and shoved himself back on the couch. Marsali was slower to move, her brain scrambling for clarity.

"Yeah, why? Have you read them?"

"No, but… I've heard things. That's the role Rikki wants for you? That's what you want to do?"

"I haven't read it yet but Rikki has never steered me wrong on a part. Why?"

"It's just… from what I've seen, the characters are very… sexual. You'd be doing that?"

"I don't know but it's just a part, Marsali."

Oh, but it wasn't. And he wasn't just an actor but her boyfriend… "May I see the script?"

Oliver snagged the script from where he'd left it and handed it to her. Marsali untangled herself from the cushions and Oliver and stood, moving several steps away from him before she randomly flipped the pages open and saw… "Oh, my word."

She skimmed the page quickly, embarrassed heat blasting through her body from the detailed description laid out on the page. Bondage. Sex toys. Spanking? "You can't do this."

"What?"

"You… Oliver, you can't seriously be thinking of… You can't take this part."

"You just said you hadn't read the books."

She held up the script to the page she'd just

read. "No, but I read this and… Oliver, really? *This* is the next best role you can get?"

His face darkened and she realized in an instant that she'd insulted him with the question. Maybe Oliver's ego wasn't impervious as she'd thought.

"What do you know about acting, Marsali? I haven't read the script yet but if Rikki says it's good, it is."

"Because of the money?"

"And other things. Marsali—"

"How much money do you need? There isn't enough money in the world for me to do something like this on-screen for millions of people to watch a-and… I don't even want to imagine what they'd do afterward."

"Do you have a problem with sex?"

"Seriously? No, I don't, but I think certain things are private and not meant to be shared."

"Rikki said it's a love story. I thought you'd be into that, if nothing else."

"Wow. Okay. No, I can't do this."

"Can't do what?"

She held the script out for him to take, aware of it shaking because of how badly she trembled. "I can't be a part of this. Any of this."

"You're giving up on us because of a part I haven't agreed to yet?"

"You want to, though. You believe Rikki's advice on doing something like this is better than me telling you it's not a good thing."

"Yeah, well, maybe if you'd actually *asked me* instead of ordering me to give up the role of my life, I might've been a little more receptive. We don't all live in Marsali's make-believe world, you know. Life gets gritty and dark. It's not all sunshine and roses. It's unrealistic."

Marsali lifted her chin and clenched her fingers at her waist, focusing on the pain of her grip rather than the pain inflicted by his words. "I'm very well aware of how dark life can be. And how sexual. But we can protect ourselves and those we love if we try."

The moment the words left her mouth, she wanted to cry. Had she really just told him she loved him? Now?

"It's a role, Marsali. Stage kisses and—"

"You're naked. *She's naked* and you're pretending to— It's triple X!" She spied Oliver's stiff countenance and knew she fought a losing battle. Only he could decide whether or not to take the part. "I want to leave."

"Marsali—"

"I'll get a cab."

"No. Just wait a sec, will you? I'll drive you. We need to talk about this."

"There's nothing more to say."

They made the drive back to her hotel in silence, and once they pulled in and a valet approached, Marsali gathered up her bag and quickly opened her door. "Don't get out."

"Marsali—"

"I need some time, Oliver. I need to think."

"Marsali, listen to me. Will you please wait?" he asked, reaching across the Jeep to grasp her arm and hold.

Her feet were out the door and she turned to glare at him. "What?"

"You're really ending this? We can't discuss it?"

She stared at him a long moment, every fiber of her being screaming to throw herself against his chest and hold tight until the outside world didn't exist anymore. But it would always intrude, and the career he held meant even if he didn't take this part, there would always be another and another. "You want to take the part."

"I want to consider it and not be told I can or

can't do something when it's my career we're discussing here."

"I understand. That's why I hope you'll understand that I *can't* be involved with something like that," she said. "Or with someone who is."

"I don't do well with ultimatums, Marsali."

She shook her head and struggled to hold back the tears burning her eyes. "It's not an ultimatum. It's… just the truth. Goodbye, Oliver."

Chapter 19

Oliver Beck Dumped By Prude!

Dumped by the Matchmaker!

Hollywood's Sexiest—Unmatched!

Her first few days home had been spent locked inside her house once more due to the pain of ending things with Oliver and the photos taken of their fight in the Jeep splashed across every tabloid and celebrity talk show with a play-by-play from the valet employee who'd been close enough to over-hear their argument. The valet reported Marsali had ended things over Oliver's potential role and she'd been dubbed a drama queen—until the role Oliver was up for was revealed and fans of her book and moral standing came out in droves to support her decision to distance herself.

Marsali stared at the headlines on her phone and wanted to crawl back in bed, pull the covers over her head, and skip the next several months as badly as the last few days.

As though conjured by her desire to stay hidden, her phone dinged, and she opened a blurry, sleep-deprived eye.

Who's the goon? Mac texted, followed by, *Let me in. Now!*

Marsali groaned and pressed her pillow to her face briefly before tossing it aside and swinging her legs to the floor. The room spun a bit due to her lack of food and prone position, so she waited several seconds before standing and stumbling her way toward her front door. She made sure to stay hidden from the reporters outside and flipped the lock. "It's okay, Denz. He's my brother."

"I want a key before I leave," Mac stated as he entered. "And full access beyond whoever that is at the door."

"Denz is security."

"Why?"

"Apparently Oliver's fan club *really* doesn't like me."

"You're getting threats?"

She shrugged. "Just a couple because they heard

I was trying to deny them the privilege of seeing Oliver naked."

Her brother took a hard look at her, his expression darkening to an even fiercer glower.

"When was the last time you showered?"

She glowered right back and shuffled her way toward the kitchen. She needed coffee. Stat. "What are you doing here?" she said, her voice croaking from lack of use and way too many self-pitying tears.

"Seriously?"

She rolled her eyes and regretted the pain it caused.

"Have you talked to Mom or Dad today?"

"It's early."

"Marse, it's one thirty in the afternoon."

"Oh." A glance at the clock on her stove proved his words true. How had that happened? "Well, you can tell them I'm fine."

"Might help if you looked it," Mac countered. "Move. I'll do it. You're making a mess."

Mac took over the coffee prep, and Marsali moved to the living room to curl up in the corner of the couch.

"I gave you three days because I knew you were jet-lagged but enough is enough. Start talking. Was that the plan?" Mac asked over his shoulder. "You and O both being raked over the coals by the tabloids because of a role? And why didn't you tell me this was happening when you picked up Ginger the night you got back? Since when do you keep important stuff from me?"

Something inside of her broke, and the faucet she thought she'd emptied into her pillow turned on again with a gush she couldn't control.

Mac turned to face her from the kitchen, a horrified expression crossing his face.

"Marse?"

"Ginger's leaving, too! They found a home for her."

"If you want her, why don't you just say you've decided to keep her?"

"Because she has to stay here alone so much. I'm a *bad* pet parent. She needs people and I've been in such a mood I told them to go ahead and place her if they have someone. They said it would be a few more days."

"You're not a bad anything. And she had you. Dogs are content with what they know, and you gave her a home, food, and love. What more could she want?"

"*Now* you tell me? It's too late!"

Mac inhaled and stared at her, hands on his hips.

"Maybe they'll change their minds. If not, you might bond with the next foster."

"I don't want another dog. Or a man," she muttered. "I mean, is it so bad that I wanted Ollie to keep his clothes on? Who wants their boyfriend getting *naked* for the world to see and doing it on-screen with some actress when we've only messed around to sec—" Marsali broke off, horrified at what she'd been about to share with her brother.

"Why would you do *anything* with Oliver when all of that was just pretend?"

Busted. Marsali squeezed her eyes shut and blamed her lack of caffeine and brain-empowering sleep for the mess she'd just made worse.

"I knew it. I *knew* he wouldn't— You wait until I get my hands on that—"

"Mac, no! It's not Ollie's fault."

"Of course it is!"

"No, it isn't. You know how I felt about him. How I've *always* felt. The stage kisses were never just… staged. Not for me." She shoved her fingers through her tangled hair and pushed it back from her face, wondering if it was possible to die of a combination of embarrassment, humiliation, and a broken heart. "And before you say anything else, I started all of this, remember? So blame me, not him."

"I knew you wouldn't be able to handle this, but I thought maybe, just maybe, you would see how different the two of you are now that he's become one of them. I thought it would help you keep your head on straight."

The rich smell of coffee filled the air around her, and she tried to inhale deeper, but her tear-sodden sinuses wouldn't allow it. "I know. It should've. But... I love him."

Silence followed her words but she didn't try to take them back.

"I know. You have for years."

She blinked and lifted her watery gaze to see Mac crossing the floor toward her. He sat on the edge of the coffee table and stared at her. "You knew?"

"Marse, why do you think I was so against this crazy idea? I've known since the first time you saw him. You looked like... I don't know, but you were wide-eyed and... That picture of you two at Mom and Dad's anniversary party held the same look you've had all these years when you're around him. Every man wants a woman to look at him the way you look at Oliver. And if he's stupid enough to give you up, that's on him."

She sniffled, the tears clearing as resignation settled deep. "Oh, Mac. What am I going to do? People hate me. Half of my client list disappeared virtually overnight since the news hit, and I'm just waiting for my editor to call and say everything is off, even though this is the type of thing my book idea covered, that of working through difficulties. Ironic, isn't it? Since we couldn't work through this?"

"Would you be okay with him acting?"

"It's who he is. Something he enjoys. I understand he'll have roles that are more… visual than others, but the series they want him to do? I'm not okay with that."

"Yeah, well, you shouldn't be. I took a look at those books and thought my brain would melt. But it'll be okay. You'll see. And I want to read those threats you've received."

She wrinkled her nose and hugged the pillow she held closer. "Denz can handle it. And they mostly yell at me for trying to hold Oliver back and ruin his career. The bodyguard is just a precaution."

"Well, I'm glad Oliver is taking them seriously

and sent the guy. I guess I have to give him credit for that."

That was something, wasn't it? That Oliver had sent Denz to her? She'd rather they'd not fought at all but… "I've had some support, too. People have started taking sides on social media and backing me, so it's not all bad."

"That's good. See? Look, just give it time for the dust to clear. Things will be back to normal soon."

"No, it won't. I've ruined everything. Oliver and me. *You* and Oliver. Nothing will ever be the same. I'm sorry, Mac."

Her brother reached out and tugged her close to hug.

"Me, too, kid. Me, too. When's Eliza coming over?"

"Why? So you can pawn the tears off on her?"

"Yup."

Marsali punched Mac for the comment and hugged him tighter.

NEARLY A WEEK after Marsali had returned to Carolina Cove, she knocked on Paul's door. The elderly man opened the main door and she smiled at him through the glass separating them. "I heard you wanted a lasagna."

Paul grinned as he pushed the storm door open and invited her inside.

"Where's your pup?"

Marsali felt tears well up and quickly blinked them away. "Home. She, um, is going to be placed in a home later today. The rescue people are coming to get her today."

"Ah, too bad. I thought maybe you'd keep her."

"I thought about it, but the company called right after I got home from California and… How have you been?"

"Better than you, I'll bet."

She made a face at his words, wondering if anyone on the face of the earth *didn't* know about her breakup with Oliver. "I'm fine, Paul." She held up the lasagna she still carried. "I just wanted to drop this off."

"Come into the kitchen," Paul said. "Stay a while and help me dig into that."

"Oh, I should get back to Ginger."

"Surely you can spare five minutes for a cup of coffee?"

The man looked so lonely Marsali didn't have the heart to turn him down. "Okay. Sure."

She followed Paul to the kitchen and sat at the table while he went to work on getting plates and utensils and the coffee he kept brewed all day.

"So you and that young man were really a thing, eh?"

"We… were," she said, still getting used to the idea of them *not* being a thing despite the days that had passed since her return. She hadn't heard from Oliver, which was disappointing, but what did she expect? The important thing was her client list had stopped falling and had swung up again, and the editor said the first three chapters she'd submitted were good and they still wanted to go to contract.

"I don't know if what the press said is true, but if it is, I'm glad you stuck to your guns, young lady. That Oliver struck me as a good man. Don't give up."

"Yes, well, I hope Oliver and I will always be friends, but I don't see us being more."

Paul set a cup of hot coffee on the table in front of her and moved to the fridge. He pulled out her favorite creamer. "When did you start drinking that?"

The man smiled and shrugged. "I decided I liked it and wanted to keep some in case I got company. My Mary always said it was important to be ready for guests. Make 'em feel welcome and they'll come."

Marsali sighed, wishing Oliver had picked up on her preferences as easily as Paul seemingly had. But then, Paul had had years to acquire the training, living with the woman he'd so adored. Not to mention her preference for coffee creamer was a long ways away from her desire to keep Oliver's naked body at least mostly to herself.

They chatted a little while longer as they drank their coffee and ate the lasagna, but as the meal went on, Paul grew quiet.

"Having a broken heart is no fun but no man worth his salt causes a woman deliberate pain. If he does, then his priorities aren't in order." He tapped his head. "Something to remember."

"Careful, Paul. You're starting to sound like my family."

"Families speak the truth more often than not, even when it's hard to hear. It's done out of love."

Marsali inhaled and stared at the man who had become a good friend in the last several years. "You're right. Oliver's life in California would've been difficult for me."

"Times have changed. Back in my day, a man had to go looking for trouble if that's what he really wanted. Today, it's everywhere you look. Or," Paul added, "part of a job. You're a level-headed woman, Marsali. Your problem," he continued, "is that you're you."

"I'm sorry?"

"Your world," Paul said, "is very different than the one your Oliver lives in and some things just can't cross."

Her stomach sank because she knew it was true. Had they been doomed from the start?

Chapter 20

Oliver tugged at the collar of the shirt he wore and prayed he could pull this off. He'd had his assistant set up the interview, but now that it was almost time to begin, his nervousness increased.

"It's time. Go to the curtains," the headset-wearing production assistant told Oliver.

Oliver made his way out of the alcove where he'd been staying out of sight and waited for the next signal.

"Ladies and gentlemen," Gwen said, "let me be honest and say it took some doing to get our next guest back on our set, and we are so glad she agreed to join us. Put your hands together and welcome professional matchmaker Marsali Jones!"

Marsali smiled and took a seat after greeting the

host. Marsali fussed with her jacket a bit before settling in, looking distinctly uncomfortable.

"But—she's not our *only* guest today. Please welcome Hollywood heartthrob Oliver Beck!"

Oliver quickly walked across the set with a hand raised to the audience, but he never took his gaze off of Marsali. He saw the color drain from her face and knew she probably expected things to go south yet again.

He greeted Gwen before moving to where Marsali sat on a love seat. He held out his hands and waited for her to place her palms in his, leaning low to kiss her on the cheek. "Breathe, Marsali."

She blinked up at him and he read the shock in her expression.

"Aren't they adorable?" Gwen said to the audience. "Marsali, you're looking a little flushed. Are you okay, dear?"

"I'm… fine."

Oliver lifted her hand to his lips. "Marsali didn't realize I was going to be here," Oliver said, staring out at the camera. "It's a surprise to her, too."

The audience cheered and whistled; a few of them jeered.

"Now, now. We just want to know what *really* happened between you two," Gwen said, smiling widely. "Oliver, tell us. How did you feel about Marsali ending things with you over what some are calling the role of a lifetime?"

"Really?" Marsali asked, her voice low and thready. "You want to do this *here*?"

The microphone she wore picked up her words, and the audience responded with applause and calls to have at it.

"Gwen, I was upset with Marsali, I'm not going to lie," Oliver said, gripping Marsali's hand tighter when she tried to pull away. "But once I calmed down, I realized she was only trying to look out for me, for us, and I knew I had some tough decisions to make."

"What kind of decisions?"

"Well, for one, I had to decide if that role *was* the best thing for me. I know it's a popular series and my fans would like to see me play the lead, but because of Marsali's upset, I questioned whether or not I should accept the role. Marsali is good at reading people, in case you don't know, and she knew instinctively that the part didn't fit me or the brand I've built over the years."

"Marsali, do you have any comment?"

"N-no," Marsali said, staring at him. "He said it w-well."

Oliver squeezed her fingers again, and for the first time since he'd arrived, Marsali's grip firmed and she held tight.

"So you won't be playing the super-sexy dominant?"

"I will not," Oliver said, shaking his head with a rueful grin. "In fact, I've spent the last week working to secure a project that takes me behind the camera rather than in front of it. It's an action series that'll be set and filmed here in Wilmington, and I'll be taking on the roles of producer and director."

Marsali's audible gasp was drowned out by those of the audience.

"Does this mean you're giving up acting?" Gwen asked.

"No. But I am going to be more selective in the acting roles I'll be taking on to focus more on indie films and the series I just mentioned so that I can spend more time on personal pursuits."

"Is this because of Marsali's upset over the nudity involved the role you were asked to play?" Gwen asked.

Oliver shook his head. "It's because when I think of the future, I don't want there to be a film my kids can't watch. Marsali opened my eyes to something I hadn't really considered, but her upset helped me see clearly that role wasn't something I'm comfortable with."

"Rumor has it you fired your agent. Is that true?"

"It is," Oliver said. "Rikki and I haven't agreed on quite a few things over the years and given the change in direction, I felt it was time to part ways."

"Marsali?" Gwen said. "What do you think?"

"I'm… I don't know what to say."

"Oliver, I think it's easy to see you've rendered Marsali and all of us speechless," Gwen said. "Would now be a good time to bring out our third guest?"

"I think it would be perfect," he said, ignored Marsali's questioning look. His assistant walked out holding Ginger's leash, and he handed the leash to Oliver.

"Ginger? How did you… What's happening?" Marsali asked.

"If you weren't going to keep her, I was," Oliver said. "Ginger is the official mascot of Beck Productions." He scooped the dog up from the floor and held Ginger close while Marsali buried her face and hands in the dog's thick fur. Ginger greeted Marsali with puppy kisses and a tail wag that shook all three of them on the love seat.

"Aww, look at that," Gwen said. "Oliver, do you have any other news to share with us?"

Oliver glanced at Marsali and smiled at the dazed expression she wore. "I hope so. But that depends on Marsali."

"What?" Marsali asked, wide-eyed.

Oliver slipped out of the seat onto one knee, pulling out a Tiffany blue box. His girl was old-school romance, and since that was the case, Tiffany was the way to go. "Marsali Jones, I love you and I want to spend my life with you. Will you marry me?"

Marsali gasped, her eyes wide on his. "Marry?"

Oliver felt his face heat in embarrassment. He should've asked her privately, just in case. "Yes. You just heard my plans. You were right. And I can't think of anything I want to do more than marry you and have that family I mentioned. So what do you say? Will you?"

Marsali stretched out her trembling fingers, her beautiful eyes glittering with tears.

"Yes. Oh, Ollie, *yes*."

Oliver slid the four-carat diamond ring on Marsali's finger and leaned forward for a very public celebratory kiss he couldn't wait to take backstage and repeat.

"You heard it here first, folks," Gwen said. "Oliver Beck put a ring on it and our hometown matchmaker is gettin' married!"

Dear Reader, I hope you enjoyed THE MATCHMAKER'S SECRET. Be sure to check out the excerpt from PERFECTLY MISMATCHED below:

"What's going on, Mac? You don't seem like yourself, and if I'm truthful, you haven't for a while."

He released her with a frown. "Nothing's going on."

"This is me, remember? I see it. I sense it. Are you really that bothered by me and Oliver making things official?"

Mac turned and lowered his arms to the top of the railing, shifting his gaze to stare out across the Cape Fear River. Two pelicans skimmed the water in the distance. "Nah. I think a part of me always knew it would happen." He shot her a teasing look. "You surprised me with the how, though," he said, referring to her very public blunder on national television when she'd outed her feelings for Oliver with an embarrassing slip of the tongue.

Marsali propped herself up beside him but faced the group seated outside the popular restaurant. Another round of laughter erupted, and he turned to look over his shoulder at the group consisting of his two neighbors and their new wives.

"There. That expression," she said. "*That's* what I'm talking about. What *is* that?"

Busted.

He lowered his chin to his chest and studied her much shorter frame. "Fine. You want to know what's wrong? I'm going to have to eat some crow, and I know it's not going to taste good."

"Oh? What happened?" she asked.

He took a fortifying breath and knew he wouldn't make it through without a lot of teasing and ribbing from his buddies—and their ladies, Marsali included. "Nothing is wrong. But here lately I've been thinking that… I'm tired of being the seventh wheel."

"The seventh… You mean with *us*?"

He watched shock roll over her features.

"Mac, please tell me we haven't made you feel unwelcome in any way."

Marsali was a sweet person. Too sweet in some ways because it made her more than a little naive and gullible. But she was always watching out for people and their feelings, checking on them, because she was such a caring person, too. She was good at reading people once she got them talking, something that helped her out a lot in her matchmaking business and the reason her dating guide had become a best-seller. "You haven't. But I think it's time you—"

"Don't you dare say you're not coming to dinner with us anymore. Or hanging out. Or… well, not doing stuff with us because we've paired up. I *mean* it!"

He chuckled at her fierceness, knowing it was born of love. "If you'd give me a chance to eat that crow I mentioned, I'd tell you I've changed my mind."

"Oh," she said, her tone filled with a little disgruntlement. "About?"

"You and"—was he really going to do this? Ready to do this?—"matchmaking."

The expression that crossed his sister's face would've been comical had it not been for the fact it was based on him placing himself and his future in her hands. As a big brother, that wasn't something easy to do on any level. After all, he was the one who should be looking out for her, not the other way around.

"You mean…?"

He groaned inwardly. She was going to make

him say it. "I mean I'm ready to throw in the towel and let you do your thing."

As a professional matchmaker with a ninety-two-percent success rate, if anyone could help him meet the right woman, she was it.

And after working nonstop to build his businesses and create a lifestyle he enjoyed, he found dating to be problematic due to the fact the women he found attractive, goal-driven, and yet family-oriented seemed to all be taken or otherwise involved.

So, if he was going to find someone to be eighth to his seventh, why not use Marsali's expertise to find a match?

"You're ready for me to *match* you?" she asked loudly, her green eyes flaring wide.

"Can we please keep this quiet? Otherwise the guys will never let me live it down."

Marsali practically jumped up and down in her excitement.

"I can't believe— Oh, my word! Yes! *Yes*, I can do this. I will find you *the* best—"

"Quietly?" he stressed.

She bit her lower lip and looked like she was going to explode from trying to contain her excitement.

"Okay, okay. I get it, but what about Mom and Dad?"

"They can't know, either. Who knows if it'll even work."

Marsali's insulted expression told him he'd gone too far.

"Excuse me, what did you just say?"

"You know what I mean. You're good at what you do, but before we celebrate another successful match, let's actually find one, shall we?"

Disgruntlement scrunched her face before she nodded with a long-suffering sigh.

"Fine. I will say this—you won't be easy. But nothing worthwhile ever is. How soon can we do the interview?"

"I'm your brother. Do we have to—"

"Oooh, yes," she said, nodding. "The interview is even *more* important with you because I can't be your sister here. I need to know *specifics* on qualities you desire, pet peeves I don't know about, looks… you name it. And you have to be honest. *Brutally* so. You can't hold back with me."

"Okay, fine. Yeah, I get it. When do you want to do this?"

"Come by my house later tonight?"

"Tonight?"

"Yes, tonight. You've *finally* agreed to let me match you. I'm not taking any chances that you'll change your mind."

KEEP READING PERFECTLY MISMATCHED!

Also, reviews help authors in immeasurable ways. I hope you'll consider leaving a review for THE MATCHMAKER'S SECRET on your favorite platform. Thank you!

MAKE ME A MATCH SERIES:

- ROMANCE RESET
- RULES OF ENGAGEMENT
- THE MATCHMAKER'S SECRET
- PERFECTLY MISMATCHED
- BY THE BOOK

MONTANA SECRETS SERIES:

- HEALING HER COWBOY
- IT HAD TO BE YOU
- HERS TO KEEP
- MILLION DOLLAR STANDOFF
- HIS CHRISTMAS WISH
- THEIR SECRET SON

THE SEASIDE SISTERS SERIES:

- THE LAST GOODBYE
- LATTES AND LULLABYES
- MAP OF DREAMS
- WORTH THE RISK
- LOST LOVE FOUND

TAMING THE TULANES SERIES:

- SMALL TOWN SCANDAL
- THEIR SECRET BARGAIN
- CROSSING THE LINE
- THE NANNY'S SECRET

- SOMEONE TO TRUST

THE STONE RIVER SERIES:

- WORTH THE WAIT
- NOT BY SIGHT
- THROUGH THE VALLEY
- LEAD ME NOT
- CHRISTMAS AT HOLLY WOOD
- THEIR CHRISTMAS MIRACLE
- SECOND CHANCES

SMALL TOWN SCANDALS SERIES:

- BRODY'S REDEMPTION
- FALLING FOR HER BOSS
- WITH THIS MAN

SECRET SANTA SERIES:

- SECRET SANTA
- SECRET SANTA II: A CHRISTMAS TO REMEMBER

MAKE ME A MATCH SERIES:

- ROMANCE RESET

Books Also Set in Carolina Cove

THE SEASIDE SISTERS SERIES:

- THE LAST GOODBYE
- LATTES AND LULLABYES
- MAP OF DREAMS
- WORTH THE RISK
- LOST LOVE FOUND

WANT TO READ OTHER BOOKS SET IN MY FICTIONAL COASTAL TOWN OF CAROLINA COVE? CHECK OUT AN EXCERPT OF THE LAST GOODBYE:

Dominic Dunn hit his turn signal and waited for a family of five to cross the sidewalk before he turned into the Carolina Cove Inn lot and parked, dread filling his stomach. Just the sight of the happy families and tourists wandering the sidewalks, lounging on restaurant patios, and enjoying the lively Saturday night left him angry. He should've ignored the letter. Ignored his next-door neighbor and best friend, ignored his boss and coworkers who said he had to honor Lisa's last request and come here.

"Mister? You gonna get out?"

The boy's voice startled Dominic and he turned to see a kid around eight years old watching him. The salt-air breeze blowing through the open windows of his car brought with it the smell of fried foods from the restaurants nearby, and seagulls squawked as they flew overhead.

"Mister?"

"Yeah," Dominic said, only then realizing he'd pulled into a parking place and was literally sitting there with his foot on the brake as he debated his choices of whether to throw the new car in reverse and floor it to get out of Carolina Cove as quickly as possible… or stay the prepaid two weeks Lisa had booked for him before her death.

"Doesn't look like it. Are you drunk?"

A rough-sounding chuckle left his chest. "Do you get a lot of drunk people here?"

"Sometimes."

"I see. Well, I'm not drunk. Just trying to decide if I want to stay here."

"Oh. You got a reservation?"

Did the kid ever stop asking questions? A memory formed, that of his son, Elijah, at the same age. "Yeah, I do."

"Then why don't you wanna stay?"

Dominic glanced at the clock and noted the time. If he left now, he'd add another six hours to his drive from Atlanta. Not how he wanted to spend what was left of the day. Maybe he should spend the night and head back to Atlanta first thing in the morning? "You've convinced me. I guess I will stay."

"I'll show you the way to the office."

"Do your parents know you're out here near the street? You're awfully young to be wandering about on your own."

The kid's shoulders squared and he lifted his chin to a defiant angle.

"I'm almost ten."

He looked younger, maybe because of his small stature. "Well, almost ten or not, there are a lot of strangers milling around, and it's not safe for kids these days. Are you visiting?" He sounded like an old man talking about "the good old days" but it was true. What kind of parent just let their kid wander the streets in a beach town full of people, some of whom probably waited on the opportunity to grab a kid and head out of town?

"No. I live here. You coming or not?"

The kid had spunk, Dominic had to give him that.

He rolled up the windows of the Porsche 911, killing the powerful engine with another press of a button. He felt a little conspicuous driving the flashy car, but he had to admit he loved the power. Just like Lisa knew he would.

He opened the door and climbed out of the low vehicle, yet another thing to get used to after driving a family-friendly SUV for so many years.

"Wow. You're tall. My mom is too. I hope I'm tall when I grow up."

Dominic locked the car and fell into step behind the boy. "I see the sign for the office. You can head home if you like."

"No. I need to check in anyway." The kid turned around and walked backward, rolling his eyes in classic kid fashion. "Or my mom will freak out and call the police again."

Again? "Does that happen a lot?"

"Her calling the police or freaking out?"

"Take your pick."

"Yeah."

Yeah to… both? Dom bit back another chuckle. Given the kid's intrepid personality, he probably kept his mom busy.

The kid flipped face-forward and Dom watched as the boy ran up the two steps leading to the office. He yanked open the door.

"Mom! Reservation!"

Dom noted the wide southern porch with its rocking chairs and a few chairs and tables before he followed the kid inside, well able to see why Lisa had liked the inn so much if the porch and office interior were anything by which to judge. It was her style of decorating. Beachy but understated.

The office walls were a soft gray with blue and sand-colored accents. There was a comfortable-looking couch and chair in the waiting area, a rope swing hanging from the ceiling in front of a painted mural of the beach and ocean behind, and on the opposite side, a coffee bar, popcorn machine, and snack area with a couple of parlor-type tables and chairs.

"Mom!"

"Samuel, how many times have I told you? No yelling. Inside voice," a woman stated as she appeared from a hallway behind the chest-high desk.

Dominic stilled, uncomfortable with the stomach-punching fact he found her beautiful. He'd guess her age to be early to mid-thirties, tall like her son said, at around five eight. Her auburn hair was scooped back and held at her nape, but curly tendrils framed her face and highlighted striking eyes that matched the blue of the ocean painting behind the check-in area.

"But, Mom, you have a reservation and sometimes don't hear me."

"A— Oh," she said, locking gazes with Dominic. "Sorry about that. Welcome to Carolina Cove Inn. I'm Ireland Cohen, the manager."

He forced himself to focus on her name rather than her beauty. "Ireland? Like the country?"

"Yes."

"Unusual name."

"Unusual family," she said by way of explanation. She flashed them both a smile. "I hope I didn't keep you waiting too long?"

"Not at all. Samuel kept me company."

"Mom, you should see his cool car! I'll bet it goes really fast. Does it?"

"It does."

"Maybe you'll take me for a ride sometime?"

"Samuel."

"I'm leaving tomorrow."

"Oh."

"And even if he wasn't, Samuel, that's not something you ask our guests. We've talked about this, remember?" the boy's mother said while sliding her son a stern glare.

"Yes, ma'am."

Samuel glanced at Dominic and rolled his eyes, and yet again Dom found himself stifling a chuckle. And wondering at the last time he'd laughed so much in such a short span of time. "Tough break, kid."

"Let's get you checked in. Name?"

"Dominic Dunn."

"Domin—"

His name ended with a gasp and Ireland's eyes filled with tears. She blinked rapidly and managed to keep them from falling, but in that instant, he knew she recognized him—and knew his reason for being there.

CLICK THE LAST GOODBYE TO KEEP READING!

About the Author

Kay Lyons always wanted to be a writer, ever since the age of seven or eight when she copied the pictures out of a Charlie Brown book and rewrote the story because she didn't like the plot. Through the years her stories have changed but one characteristic stayed true— they were all romances. Each and every one of her manuscripts included a love story.

Published in 2005 with Harlequin Enterprises, Kay's first release was a national bestseller. Kay has also been a HOLT Medallion, Book Buyers Best and RITA Award nominee. Look for her most recent novels with Kindred Spirits Publishing.

For more information regarding her work, please visit Kay at the following:

www.kaylyonsauthor.com

@KayLyonsAuthor (Twitter)

Kay Lyons Author (Facebook)

Author_Kay_Lyons (Instagram)

Kay Lyons, Author (Pinterest)

SIGN UP FOR KAY'S NEWSLETTER AND RECEIVE UPDATES ON NEW RELEASES, CONTESTS, PRE-RELEASE BOOK INFORMATION, EXCLUSIVES AND MORE!

FAQ

Is Carolina Cove a real place?

Carolina Cove is purely fictional; however, it is *loosely* based on one of my favorite places—Kure Beach, North Carolina. Kure Beach is home to a wonderful pier, a pavilion for special events like weddings and birthdays, swings facing the Atlantic, pelicans Pete and George, coffee shops, restaurants, and more. It's also close to the North Carolina Aquarium, Carolina Beach, and Wilmington.

Can I stay at the Carolina Cove Inn?

While Carolina Cove and the Carolina Cove Inn are purely fictional, there are plenty of motels and rentals in the area to enjoy.

But the pier is real?

Yes! And it has quite a history. Be sure to check out the Kure Beach Pier Cam for a view of Kure Beach and the Atlantic.

What about the restaurants and coffee shops and places you've mentioned in the series?

London's Lattes is based on two of my favorite local coffee shops in Kure Beach and Carolina Beach. Are there more? Yes, plenty. But those two shops I know well because I've visited fairly often while writing these stories. Neither of them on their own was perfect for what I had in mind for London's, however, so I basically combined the two and ta-da! London's Lattes was born. But, no, if you go into either of them, you won't find London's exact business. Isn't fiction wonderful?

Why make up a city? Why not use Kure Beach?

One of the best things about writing fiction is that when a story appears a certain way, you can write it just that way. Carolina Cove and the characters appeared to me in story form and while Kure Beach IS one of my favorite places, I had to change some things to better fit the series as well as steer far away from any real-life persons/families for obvious reasons. Doing so, that meant also changing the name of the city, etc. But, that said, you will find a slew of similarities in the fictional city and the real one. :)

Where is the dream catcher mailbox?

Unfortunately the dream catcher mailbox is pure fiction and an idea taken from a "beach mailbox" I visited once many years ago. The dream catcher mailbox first appeared in the SEASIDE SISTERS SERIES.

How did you research the matchmaking aspect?

Oh, the answer to this was fun! Wilmington actually has a professional matchmaker. I interviewed her to get my details straight and learned a lot about a very fascinating business!

MAKE ME A MATCH SERIES:

- ROMANCE RESET
- RULES OF ENGAGEMENT
- THE MATCHMAKER'S SECRET
- PERFECTLY MISMATCHED
- BY THE BOOK